A LIFE NAIVE

Gray Door Ltd.

ISBN 978-1-945530-92-0

Contents

Chapter One: Life, Death and Change

Hershel dipped the tea bag into a cup of hot water. He examined the liquid carefully. When the tea was just right, he pulled the bag out and then placed one spoonful of sugar in and stirred it.

After placing the cup of tea and several cookies onto a tray, the young man carefully carried it through the large old house and into a sitting room.

"Here's your tea and cookies, Me'ma."

An elderly lady sat in a large chair and watched closely as Hershel moved beside her.

"Yes, I can see what you have, Hershel; set it down there." She replied.

Once the tray was on the table beside her, Hershel sat in a chair across from his grandmother. She sipped her tea and then took a small bite of a cookie. Then she looked at her grandson.

"I need you to go by the bank and the post office after you take the Lincoln to have it serviced. Also, the lawn needs to be cut, it's beginning to look like a jungle out there."

"Yes, Me'ma."

His grandmother picked up a sealed letter and several other items from a side table. Then handed them to Hershel.

"Mail this letter, and remember 'certified mail.' Also bring me the receipt, don't set it down somewhere and forget about it."

Looking over the items, he examined the letter carefully.

"Another letter for Mr. Nelson?"

"Yes, it's another letter for Mr. Nelson."

"Are you and Mr. Nelson going to get married, Me'ma?"

Hershel's grandmother laughed a bit. "No, most certainly not; Mr. Nelson is a business associate. I'm much to old for anything such as that."

"How old are you, Me'ma?"

"Well, let's see. It's May of 1962 and I was born in March of 1890, so it seems I'm 72 now." She then picked her tea back up.

After taking a sip, she studied Hershel for a few seconds. "Hershel, have you noticed Miss Wesley down at the bank? She's quite pretty. I believe she's close to your age; around twenty-six or twenty-seven."

Hershel appeared startled by this question. He fidgeted a few moments and replied in a soft voice. "Yes, I've seen Miss Wesley, Me'ma. She is very pretty."

"Well, you should ask her out. From what I understand, she's from a respectable St. Louis family and would make a wonderful wife, I'm sure."

Hershel again fidgeted and shifted in his chair.

"You mean, ask her out on a date?"

His grandmother's face twisted slightly in a frustrated manner. She stared at her grandson as he appeared very uncomfortable.

"Yes, I mean ask her out on a date. Hershel, you're twenty-seven years old. I'm not going to be around forever. You should find a nice girl and get married."

"Don't say that, Me'ma. You keep saying that. I don't want anything to happen to you."

"I don't wish for anything to happen to me either. But eventually, I will pass away. You should be prepared for that."

Hershel looked away from his grandmother. He stared at the floor and clasped his hands together nervously.

"I'll do those errands for you now, Me'ma." He stood up and his grandmother nodded.

"Remember what I said about Miss Wesley. You really should ask her out on a date. You're welcome to use the Lincoln and take her to one of those... drive in movies, if you like."

Hershel stepped towards the doorway, "Yes Me'ma, I'll think about it."

The young man went out to the garage and climbed into the large, dark blue, Lincoln Continental. He enjoyed going on errands for his grandmother. He started the car and was soon on his way.

He went by the service station and drank an Orange Crush soda as the attendant serviced the car.

Then he went by the post office. After mailing the letter, he stopped and talked with Gerald Mavis, the owner of a local hardware store.

At the bank he handed the withdrawal slip his grandmother had given him to Miss Wesley. She smiled and began counting out the bills. He tried to speak to her but couldn't summon the courage. She placed the money into an envelope and said "thank you, Mr. Lawson."

"Thank you, Miss Wesley," he replied and left the bank.

Back at the grand old house, his grandmother's Doctor had arrived for a weekly visit. After laying his suit jacket on the back of a chair, he sat down across from Hershel's grandmother.

"So how are you feeling today, Ethel?"

"How do you think, Doctor Gregory? I'm the same as last week and the week before. Other than this faltering heart, I'm as fit as can be. Are you certain I must relax all the time. I hate sitting around, simply waiting to die."

Doctor Gregory smiled with compassion, "Ethel, you don't have to think of it that way."

"Well, I'm not going to sugar coat it either. You're the one that said my heart could stop at any time. What I want to know is, does it really matter if I sit around and 'take it easy' as you put it, or if it will simply quit at some point regardless."

Doctor Gregory readjusted himself in the chair. He leaned forward slightly as he spoke to her. "I can't say anything for certain, Ethel. But I feel confident in telling you, the more exertion or excitement you place on your heart, the more likely you can have cardiac failure. It's really your choice. I'm not trying to condemn you to sitting around, bored and unhappy, but rather I'm telling you the situation and you can act according to that information."

Ethel reacted as if hearing bitter news. But she quickly recovered and replied politely, "Thank you, Doctor. I know you're simply doing your job and I appreciate that."

Doctor Gregory leaned back in his chair and clasped his hands together. "So, what about your grandson, Hershel; have you told him yet?"

Again she reacted as if uncomfortable. "I've tried to tell Hershel. He just doesn't want to hear anything that has to do with me dying. He's a sensitive boy and it's rather difficult to just 'say it.' I'm not sure how he would handle it."

"He's twenty-seven years old, Ethel. I realize he's sensitive, but otherwise there's nothing wrong with him. He's been sheltered since he was a young boy. He'll have to face it one way or another, sooner or later."

"Yes, yes I know that. But you must understand, Doctor, Hershel was traumatized when he was young. His mother, my son's wife, was not a capable woman. After Hershel's father was killed in an unfortunate, work related accident, his mother simply fell apart. She left Hershel and his older brother alone in the house for days at a time. I had no idea this was going on or I could have intervened sooner. I arrived at their house one day to find the boys alone and searching the cabinets for something to eat. The house was a mess and young Hershel was in a poor emotional state."

Ethel paused and stared out over the room. She seemed to be talking to herself as much as telling the Doctor the story. She took a deep breath and continued.

"I brought the boys home with me and when I talked with their mother she said it was best. She just couldn't handle the responsibility alone. I have no idea where she is these days.

"Hershel's brother, Joe Jr. has handled the situation much better than his younger brother. I placed them both in the school here and Joe did alright, but Hershel struggled, being in a class full of other children. It seemed to cause him to withdraw even more. So I took him out and hired a private tutor. His brother was not very understanding about this and has been somewhat abrasive to him over the years.

"Joe graduated school and went off to college. But Hershel stayed here with me, hovering about like a 'mother hen.' I've tried to

4

encourage him to get out and live, but he's been reluctant to do so. He's a good boy, and I'm reluctant to tell him about my condition. I really don't see that it would help anything."

Doctor Gregory nodded. He thought of the situation briefly and then asked, "what about his brother Joe. Will he be able to stay with him... I mean once...?"

Ethel grunted, "no I don't believe so. And if he were to stay with him it wouldn't be mutually beneficial. Joe has a family and stays busy with his work. He's the picture of a competent, and confident family man. But, he wouldn't have the patience to deal with Hershel, even if he agreed on his brother staying with him."

She briefly paused in thought, then continued.

"And, as it is, I sincerely doubt that Hershel could handle a large amount of money, or property. Particularly if he were put in a difficult situation. His brother, on the other hand, is very shrewd in matters of money and finances.

"No, I've made a difficult decision concerning the two, and though I'm sure it's far from perfect, it's what must be done. There is simply no substitute for hard work, dedication and self sacrifice for family."

She now looked at the Doctor, seeming to want a response. He considered her words but finally said, "You've raised them both, Ethel. I'm sure you know what's best."

After Doctor Gregory said this, the front door was heard opening and soon Hershel came to the sitting room.

"Hello Doctor Gregory."

"Hello Hershel." The Doctor replied.

Hershel then handed several items to his grandmother.

"Thank you, Hershel," she said.

Several days later, Hershel brought his grandmother her tea and sugar cookies. As he was about to leave the room she stopped him.

"Hershel, please have a seat. I would like to talk with you."

"What is it, Me'ma?"

His grandmother took a deep breath. "Hershel, you know that I care for you and your brother both, don't you?"

Hershel looked at her with obvious confusion. "Yes, I know that Me'ma. Why would you ask such a thing?"

"Well, there may come a time when you... perhaps won't understand decisions I've made. Decisions concerning you and your brother." She paused in thought and then continued. "Joe has a family and though he can be, well, a little abrasive at times, he is a hard worker and takes care of his family. He is also very shrewd in financial matters. There will be a time that you must take these things into consideration." She grimaced slightly as if foreseeing this time. Then she continued.

"Hershel, you are a fine young man, but I just don't feel that you are ready to deal with certain things, things which your brother has become very... frugal at. There will be a time that you may not initially understand my decisions, but I hope you will trust that I've tried to make wise and prudent choices concerning you and your brother. Will you remember that?"

"Yes, I'll remember that, Me'ma. But what's this about?" Hershel appeared completely puzzled by the conversation.

"Well, it's not important right now. It's just something that I felt I needed to tell you. You can go now."

Later that evening, Hershel turned the television on and watched his favorite show. Then, after checking on his grandmother, he took a hot bath and went to bed.

The following morning he followed his regular routine. After eating and preparing breakfast for his grandmother, he finally got the small yard mowed with a push mower.

Hershel never thought much beyond one day to the next. He was content with this type of routine. Days passed by in a safe and secure manner. He would always find something to do around the place and enjoyed the quiet life.

Every time he went to the bank, he would try to talk to Miss Wesley, and every time he would lose his courage. Every few days he would go grocery shopping or mail letters and buy stamps for his grandmother. He would almost always have the Lincoln filled with gasoline on Thursdays. His favorite television shows came on Friday evenings and every Sunday after church service he would get a vanilla ice cream soda from the drug store.

But, for Hershel everything was about to change. His world was about to suddenly evaporate and it would never be the same again.

"Good morning, Me'ma, here's your breakfast." He sat the tray down on the small table beside his grandmother's bed and then went to the windows and opened the curtains.

"I think the paperboy threw the paper in the hedge again." He then carefully examined the front lawn through the windows.

Light streamed into the bedroom from the open curtains. He glanced back at his grandmother. She lay motionless in bed. Her sleeping mask still covering her eyes.

"Me'ma, your breakfast is ready."

Hershel suddenly felt very odd. He stared at his grandmother and a thought came to his mind. It was a thought he had ignored and refused to face for many years now. He walked slowly over to his grandmother's bed.

"Me'ma... are you awake?"

He pulled a chair over and sat down beside the bed. He looked at her with wide eyes. He felt as if he couldn't breathe. His heart began to beat rapidly in his chest.

"Me'ma... Me'ma, your breakfast is ready."

Still his grandmother lay motionless. He slowly reached over and touched her hand. It was cold. He moved his hand back to his lap. He sat staring at his dead grandmother. He didn't know what to do.

For what seemed like an hour, Hershel sat staring at his Me'ma. Finally, he picked up the tray and went downstairs. He called Doctor Gregory and then went into the sitting room. He sat and stared at the wall until the Doctor arrived.

For the next few days, Hershel felt as if he was floating helplessly in an ocean of activity. His grandmother had prepared everything for this time and it was as if Hershel now became a spectator, as others took care of his grandmother.

At the service, he sat in the front of the funeral home. A beautiful urn with his grandmothers ashes sat on a small table. A nice photograph of her sat beside the urn. People came and went as Hershel stared blankly at the urn. They would pat him on the back before leaving. A few would say, "she was a wonderful woman."

The big house felt very empty now. But then, Hershel's brother, Joe, and his family arrived for the reading of the will.

"Hershel! Hey there brother, it's good to see you." Joe smiled and shook Hershel's hand as he entered the house. His wife Linda and their son JJ came in behind Joe.

"The place hasn't changed a bit." Joe walked to the sitting room as Linda and JJ followed. Hershel closed the front door and went to the sitting room.

Joe was sitting in the chair his grandmother usually sat in. Linda sat down at a small love seat and JJ began snooping around the room.

"I sure hated to hear about Grandma. But that's what happens to old people, I suppose."

Hershel sat down as Joe said this. Joe then continued.

"I guess all those years of waiting on the old gal, hand and foot, will finally pay off for you now, eh Hershel?" Joe sort of winked at his brother and then gazed around the sitting room. He then continued before Hershel could reply.

"Yeah I figure she left everything to you. I was surprised when the lawyer called me. But hey, I guess old Grams had a soft spot in her heart for little Joey after all."

Joe then leaned over towards Hershel. "We figure she gave us the Lincoln. Do you happen to know how many miles it has on it?"

Hershel shook his head a little, "Uhm, no I don't know, Joe."

Something fell in the corner of the room and broke. Hershel turned, a bit startled to see that JJ had knocked a vase off it's table.

"JJ, leave stuff alone!" Linda shouted in a high voice that also startled Hershel.

"Sorry about that. He's just curious about everything right now. You know, ten years old and wants to take everything apart and put it back together... It's the putting back together that he has problems with." Joe then laughed.

"Well, it's alright, I guess. Are you all staying here tonight?" Hershel asked and then noticed JJ opening a curio cabinet, and investigating the knick-knacks inside.

"Yeah we're staying here, Hersh. You think we got the money to stay in a hotel? You may have that sort of money now, but we're still on a budget."

Hershel nodded and replied with a bewildered voice, "alright, I'll get some blankets for the spare rooms." He then stood up and made his way out of the sitting room just as something from the curio cabinet fell on the floor.

"JJ, dang it all, I told you to leave stuff alone!"

Hershel cringed again as Linda shouted out to her son. He continued upstairs to the spare rooms and prepared the beds. Afterwards he cooked a meal and cleaned up while the guests got ready for bed.

The next day they got dressed and ready to go downtown for the reading of the will. As they went outside Joe turned to his wife Linda. "I think I'll ride with Hershel, Hon. You and JJ just follow us." He then turned to Hershel. "You won't run off and leave her will you, Hersh?"

"No, I don't drive over the speed limit. I won't go too fast."

After Linda and JJ loaded into their car, Hershel backed the Lincoln Continental out of the garage. Once out, he stopped so Joe could get in.

"Yeah, this is a beauty. Love these Lincolns. That's one thing about Grams, she had a sense of style."

Joe then leaned over towards Hershel as he put the car in reverse.

"How many miles does this thing have on it?" He inspected the odometer and then replied quickly, "oh that's not bad, not bad at all. I guess you and Grams only drove this thing around town right?"

Hershel glanced at his brother. He didn't like Joe calling his grandmother 'Grams,' but he didn't say anything. Instead he answered the question as they started towards the lawyers office.

"Well, Me'ma hasn't driven the car for several years. She didn't feel well enough."

Joe laughed out loud after hearing this. He tried to stifle his obvious amusement, but could barely do so.

"Me'ma... I forgot you called her that! Oh, I'm sorry Hersh, I just can't believe you still call her that... So, eehmphtt.. so, 'Me'ma' didn't mind you calling her that?' Joe again chuckled in a sarcastic manner.

Hershel glanced at his brother as he tried to also focus on the road.

"Well, I suppose she didn't mind. She never said anything about it."

Joe calmed down some now. He seemed to put forth an effort to become serious.

"Yeah, well I'm sure she didn't mind, Hersh. And uhm, I'm sorry for laughing about that. It really is sweet that you still called her that."

Joe glanced out the window and moved about in the car seat as if a little nervous. He then turned to Hershel.

"Listen, Hersh, uhm... well uh. It's uhm... Well listen, I know Grandmother probably left most everything to you. And I understand that. I mean you hung around and took care of her and all that."

Joe scratched the side of his head as Hershel again glanced at his brother. He then continued, as if not sure what he wanted to say.

"Well, you see Hershel, it's just that, well, it's like I was telling Grams on the phone a while back, I got a family and all. You know, JJ... oh that boy, you wouldn't believe it, Hersh. That JJ he goes through shoes almost ever week it seems. You just wouldn't believe how much it costs to keep him in clothes.

"And don't even ask about the cost to feed him. He eats like a horse! And then Linda has this, well it's, a medical thing. The Doctor bill is, well, it's real high. Anyway, I could really use some help. I mean, we're family right?"

Hershel turned a corner and then briefly looked at Joe.

"Yes, we're family, you're my brother."

Joe laughed and patted Hershel on the arm.

"That's great, Hersh, I knew you would understand. And listen, you know, just two or three thousand ought to be enough... Well, I mean it depends on how much Grams left you. You know, we could use more and if she left you a lot, then surely you could spare a little more..." He laughed again, "or a lot more... I mean if she left you a lot. Who knows how much old Grams was worth, right?"

Joe smiled and chuckled again as Hershel glanced at him apprehensively.

"This is great, Hersh, I knew you would understand and help out. I told Linda, 'he's my brother and he'll share with his own flesh and blood brother.'"

As Joe was saying this they pulled into the parking lot of the lawyer's office.

Once they were all inside, Joe looked around. The lawyer sat down and Joe blurted out, "so this is it? Just us?"

The lawyer was a man of around sixty years old. He had black framed glasses and appeared slightly irritated by Joe's outburst.

As he got comfortable in his chair the lawyer started to answer Joe, "yes, you are..." He then looked at JJ and stopped in mid-sentence. The young boy was very focused on the task of picking his nose. In fact, he had his finger so far up his nose that he seemed to notice nothing else.

Joe, Linda and Hershel were all watching and listening to the lawyer. Now they turned their attention to JJ and immediately Linda swatted the boy's hand away from his nose.

"Hey... what??" The boy said as his mother growled at him.

The lawyer straightened his glasses and proceeded. "You are the only ones designated in your grandmother's will."

Hershel noticed Linda smile wide and clasp Joe's hand in anticipation.

The reading of the will commenced. "To my grandson Joseph Lawson I bequeath my house and all belongings other than those designated to my grandson Hershel. Also the remainder of funds in my bank account."

At this point Linda began to moan, almost as if having a sexual experience. Her eyes were wide and she was leaning forward.

The lawyer held a check up and continued, "the funds come to the amount of seventeen thousand, three hundred, seventy two dollars, and thirteen cents."

Joe jumped up and shouted out in joy. Linda screamed out loud and then began to laugh. The two hugged each other, then Joe grabbed the check out of the lawyers' hand. He looked it over as Linda also held her hand to her mouth and stared at the check."

"And the house right?? She left us the house? You said she left me the house, Joseph Lawson?"

The lawyer now expressed much irritation but remained calm. "That is correct, the house goes to Joseph Lawson."

Joe and Linda again jumped up and down while hugging each other. Then Joe appeared to think of something.

"Wait a minute.. What did she leave him?" He pointed at Hershel who sat watching the events with very little emotion.

Joe then turned to Linda. "She probably left the real money to him."

The elderly lawyer expelled another loud breath through his nose, "yes, well, if we could have a minute of calm, I'll continue."

Joe and Linda sat down and listened intently.

"To my grandson, Hershel Lawson, I leave my 1958 Lincoln Continental. Also, Hershel is to have first choice of any items from my house that he wishes to have, as long as they fit in the Lincoln. I also leave Hershel seven hundred dollars cash. My final request is that my grandson, Hershel, use this money and drive my ashes, in the Lincoln, to a mausoleum prepared for the remains. The mausoleum is in Los Angeles California. I have made all the preparations with the cemetery director and he will be expecting my remains to be delivered by Hershel."

12

Joe and Linda looked at each other. Linda stifled a laugh and then turned away. Joe was obviously amused, but pretended to be serious.

"Well, Hersh, you got the Lincoln after all, Buddy. I'm a little jealous about that. That's a sweet car, and low mileage."

The lawyer stared at Joe as he once again adjusted his glasses. He then reached into his desk and pulled out an envelope. "Here's the seven hundred dollars cash, Hershel."

Hershel took the envelope. "Thank you."

Outside the office, Joe and Linda laughed and looked at the check again and again. Hershel walked to the Lincoln and watched until they had loaded into their car, then they left in an obvious hurry.

When Hershel arrived back at the house, Joe and Linda's car was parked in the single car garage. Hershel parked the Lincoln on the side of the road.

As he walked up to the front door, he could hear his brother speaking very loudly. Upon opening the screen door, he saw that Joe was on the telephone.

"Yeah, the whole house and everything in it! Oh, it's incredible, we can't believe it! Yeah, I know... Well, at least another week. I'll contact an auction firm today and get the ball rolling."

Joe noticed Hershel and sort of waved and smiled. He then turned away and continued his conversation. "Yeah, well I'll owe you some days, Frank. Listen I'll make it up on Saturdays, if need be. I'll get this place sold in a jiffy and be back to work as soon as possible... Yeah, this is a big deal. This is going to get those bill collectors off our backs for good... Yeah, yeah, sure, JJ's college, you bet."

As Hershel walked upstairs, he heard Linda squeal or almost scream. He stopped at the very top of the stairs, but where he could still see Joe below on the phone. Linda came running from Hershel's grandmothers' room. She held a necklace in her hands and Joe put his hand over the phone as she approached him.

"Look at this! real diamonds, and pure gold! She had a whole jewelry box full of this stuff! Gold, diamonds, pearls, it's got to be worth a fortune!"

"Shhh..." Joe said, as he glanced around, but didn't notice Hershel standing at the top of the stairs.

"Hershel gets first pick! Anything he can put in that old Lincoln is his." He again looked around and in a lower voice continued. "Hide the box somewhere, or better yet, put it in the trunk of our car later."

Linda nodded and went back to the room holding the necklace down, as if hiding it. Joe then continued his conversation on the phone as Hershel moved on down the hallway.

Hershel sat down on his bed. He stared at the floor and listened to Joe and his family rummaging around downstairs. A little later, he heard the trunk of Joe's car open and moving to the window saw Linda and Joe carrying boxes into and out of the garage. A few minutes later, Linda again came out with an arm full of what looked to be his grandmother's antique silverware and some other objects. Again Hershel heard the trunk of their car open and close.

As Hershel lay down on his bed, he continued to hear movements downstairs. He stared at the ceiling until drifting off to sleep.

The next morning he was somewhat shocked to walk out of his room and find stuff pulled out into the hallway. Boxes had been extracted from closets and the ladder to the attic was pulled down. Hershel stepped up the ladder far enough to see Joe going through everything with a flashlight.

Stepping back down, Hershel had to navigate around items stacked on the stairs. Again in the first floor hallway he found household furniture and storage boxes strewn about. He carefully made his way to the kitchen, past a spare room where Linda and JJ were busy searching through miscellaneous items pulled from a closet. It appeared they had a small stack of choice pieces already gathered together in the middle of the room.

In the kitchen, Hershel found a mess of dirty dishes by the sink and littered about the table. He prepared himself a bowl of cereal and quietly ate it.

After breakfast he began cleaning while noises in the house sounded as if it were being torn apart. Before he was completely finished washing the dishes a knock was heard on the front door.

Hershel briefly turned his attention away from the sink. He heard what sounded like Linda stumbling over stuff and then finally answering the door. A few seconds later she yelled out towards the upstairs and attic.

"Joe.... There's a Mr. Thompson here to see you. He's from the auction company."

Soon a noise could be heard as if Joe were also stumbling downstairs and thru a maze of boxes and assorted items.

Hershel turned his attention back to the dishes. Several minutes later and after some talking up front, it seemed as if Joe were moving up and then back down the stairs. His brother eventually entered the kitchen, a bit winded.

"Oh, there you are Hersh. I thought you were still asleep. Listen, there's a man here that needs to get an idea of what all will be auctioned off. I told him you was going to pick a few things out first, you know like Grams wanted you to do. Do you suppose you could do that real quick?"

Hershel began drying his hands on a towel.

"Uhm, I guess so. I'll need to take some luggage when I take Me'ma to California, so I don't think I can take a whole lot."

Joe expressed excitement about this and immediately perked up.

"That's right, good thinking! You don't want to forget your own things. Maybe you can pick a few small items, real quick like. You know, some sentimental stuff. Pictures maybe. You like pictures right? Come on, I'll help you."

Joe took him by the arm and lead him past a man in a suit, which Hershel thought to be Mr. Thompson. They were soon in the sitting room, where a hint of moth balls lingered in the air. It appeared as if a bomb had exploded as stuff was strewn everywhere.

In the middle was a stack of items such as paintings from the walls, the contents from the curio cabinet and a number of intricately carved ivory boxes that Hershel remembered his Me'ma saying came from Africa.

Around the edges were other piles of items such as family pictures and furniture covers. These items appeared to be of little value.

Hershel began to look closer at the ivory boxes in the middle of the room. There were five of them in the set and they were large to small. His Me'ma told him they would fit into each other. When Joe saw him looking at the boxes, he took Hershel's arm again and pulled him over to the pictures that had been taken down and were on the floor leaning against the wall.

"Hey, over here Hersh. We're looking for pictures right? Here we go, here's some of Grams... I mean Me'ma. And here's a few with Gramps in them as well. Oh look, here's one when we were boys, after Me'ma brought us here, you'll want that one for sure."

Joe then yelled out past Hershel, "Linda, bring a box! Hurry, Hershel wants to take some pictures with him to California!"

Joe's voice was so loud that Hershel briefly put a finger to his ear. Soon Linda was running in with a box.

"Go get JJ would you, Hon; he can be loading this into the Lincoln while I help Hershel pick his stuff out." Joe then patted his brother on the arm, "not too much though, gotta have some room for your clothes and such right?"

Joe hastily put a mixed bag of a dozen or so framed pictures in the box. "JJ come here son. Run this box out to your uncle Hershel's Lincoln. And get another box on your way back."

JJ took the half-full box out to the street and placed it in the back seat of the Lincoln, while Joe ushered Hershel around the room.

"Oh, Hersh, here's Grams footstool. You'll want to keep that. I would love to take it as a keep sake, but it would just get broken at my house. You know how young boys can be on furniture..." He then looked around for his son.

"JJ, run this footstool out to Uncle's car."

16

After a few more random items were cast into a box and young JJ ran them out to the car, Joe quickly closed the process for Hershel, who hadn't said much of anything at all.

"Well that's probably all you can take, Hersh... and still have room for your clothes and personal stuff." Joe then almost pushed Hershel back out and into the hallway.

After Hershel was back in the kitchen, he heard Joe searching for Mr. Thompson.

"Oh, there you are Mr. Thompson, we're ready now, my brother has everything he wants." After Joe said this, the two began moving through the house and Mr. Thompson busily made notes while also telling Joe what needed to be done before the auction.

Hershel stayed in his room and out of the way as Mr. Thompson's assistants soon arrived and also began separating items in preparation for the sale.

For the next two days Hershel continued to stay hidden as everything in the house was pulled out and examined, cleaned up and placed into different areas of the structure. On the third day there came a knock at the door. Hershel was in his room but still heard it.

"Hershel, can you come down please?" Linda's loud tenor voiced boomed all the way upstairs.

Stepping down the stairs, Hershel could see a man standing on the porch, holding an odd rectangular shaped case. Linda stood looking at it with a sour look on her face.

"Hershel, this man is here with....." She pointed at the case as if it were a snake, her face grimacing.

"Mr. Hershel Lawson, I'm here with your grandmother's ashes." The man lifted the case up slightly and then continued. "You're grandmother has ensured that specific instructions have been followed concerning her remains. This case and urn are to be hand delivered to the cemetery's director once you reach Los Angeles."

"Uhm, okay. When do I need to get her there?" Hershel asked the man as Linda left the area quickly.

"There's no set time, Mr. Lawson. But I would imagine the sooner the better. The case will protect the remains for the most part. But you should get them to their final resting place as soon as you're able to."

Hershel nodded in agreement as the man handed him the case. He then thanked the man and returned upstairs with his grandmother's remains. Soon after this, there was a knock on his door. He opened it to find Joe.

"Hey Hersh, you got Grams ashes now huh? I guess you'll be wanting to get on the way soon then? Yeah, we're just going to get things settled up with the house and stuff; then we'll be on the way too. So... when are you leaving?"

Hershel considered the question. Joe raised his eyebrows and then turned his head a little in anticipation.

"I'm not sure. I've never been to California."

"Oh, it's no problem getting to California. You just go south a few miles until you hit highway 66, then follow it on out to the west coast. No problem at all. I've heard it's a great drive. You'll love it. That big old Lincoln will take you there in no time at all."

"Really?" Hershel asked with a bit of disbelief.

"Sure, you'll love it. I wish I could go with you, but I need to get this business with the house settled and then get back to work. It'll be great though... the wind blowing through your hair." Joe moved his hand as if laying out the scene for his brother. "Open spaces and beautiful views. You'll go by the Grand Canyon, Hersh, boy oh boy I wish I could see that!"

Hershel thought about this as Joe seemed to be waiting for an answer.

"Yeah, I guess I'll get packed and go in a day or two."

"There you go, that's the spirit. You have your mission soldier and it's a mission to have fun!" Joe then acted as if he were punching Hershel in the chest, but then patted him on the arm. 'You need any help packing? I can send JJ up."

"No, I think I can get it."

18

"Alrighty then, you know, if you get to it, you might be able to get out of here tomorrow. You could, avoid some of the weekend traffic!"

Joe then went downstairs where Linda promptly and with a loud voice asked him when Hershel was leaving.

That night Hershel packed several bags with clothes and necessities. The next morning he ate breakfast and as he began packing his bags in the Lincoln, Joe pulled up with a small, rental moving truck. He backed it into the driveway and then came over to Hershel.

"Well, looks like your getting ready to go! I sure envy you. But it's just not the same when you have a family. A guy can't take off on an exciting and fun filled drive whenever he wants if he has a family. I guess that's why Grams picked you for the job."

Hershel put his bag in the back seat and shut the car door. "Yeah, I suppose so."

Well, good luck then, Hersh. You'll have to send us some post cards."

After Joe said this, Linda came out the front door with a box in her arms and yelled, "hurry up Joe, we need to get the furniture loaded before the auction people come back!"

"Yeah, yeah, I'll be right there." Joe then turned back to Hershel. "Just loading a few things we'll be taking home."

For a brief instant, Joe's eyes expressed compassion for Hershel. He reached back and got his wallet out. "Hey, uhm, here's a little something." He pulled a fifty dollar bill half way out, but then tucked it back in and pulled a twenty dollar bill out. He handed it to Hershel and, rather reluctantly it seemed, pulled another five dollar bill out and handed it to his brother.

"There's a little sock money for the trip."

Hershel looked at the twenty-five dollars in his hand. "Sock money?"

"Yeah, sock money. You know, you put it in your sock just in case of an emergency." Joe smiled and patted Hershel on the arm. "I gotta go. You be careful now, you hear?"

Hershel nodded as he held the money and watched Joe jog back to the large dwelling. He then stood and looked at the house as if it might say bye to him. After a few reminiscent moments, he reached down and placed the folded twenty-five dollars into his sock. Then Hershel got in the Lincoln and drove towards highway 66.

Chapter Two: Route 66

After winding through St. Louis a ways, the large Lincoln Continental was soon cruising with ease through the Missouri countryside. Hershel would occasionally glance over to the passenger seat where he had placed his grandmother's ashes.

The warm, fragrant summer breeze filtered through his hair and Hershel thought his brother Joe was certainly right. This would be a nice drive to the west coast.

As evening set in, Hershel stopped at a quaint little motel for the night. The room was tiny, but clean. There was a cafe next to the motel and after a meal and bath he slept soundly until dawn.

Early the following morning Hershel ate breakfast. As the sun was clearing the horizon he pulled back onto highway 66 heading west. His wallet began to bother his hip, so he reached over to the glove box and tossed it in. This made things more comfortable and he settled back into the seat as more Missouri scenery passed by.

Around one o'clock Hershel pulled into a small town. He found a gas station that had a cafe next door. As the attendant filled the car with gas and Hershel went to the restroom, a man in a checkered suit watched him with interest from across the street.

Hershel paid for the fuel and then pulled the Lincoln next door to the cafe. He walked inside and had a seat.

"I'll be right with you, Darlin." A waitress called out to him as he sat. Hershel waved to her and then looked around the small establishment. It had a cozy feeling and the wonderful fragrance of food drifted about.

Several minutes later the waitress had taken Hershel's order and he was sipping his soda through a straw.

The man dressed in a checked suit came into the cafe. He appeared to be around forty years old and had his hair slicked back. He was carrying a suitcase and walked towards Hershel, but seemed to be looking for a place to sit. He glanced down to Hershel and stopped.

"Harold... Harold Madlock, what are you doing here, you old badger?" The man in the checkered suit patted Hershel on the back and quickly sat down across from him as if ready for a long discussion.

"Excuse me?" Hershel said with a bit of shock.

"Harold, don't you remember me? The convention in Chicago, two years ago? Come on Harold, how could you forget a night like that. I mean, I had a hangover for a week, but we painted the town red. You telling me you forgot me already, Buddy?"

Hershel looked back to see if there was someone behind him. When he realized the man was really talking to him he almost stuttered a response.

"I.. uhm, I'm not Harold. My name is Hershel, Hershel Lawson."

The man examined Hershel very closely. "You got to be kidding me... No, you're not Harold are you? I can't believe it. You're the spitting image of my buddy Harold. That's uncanny."

At this point the waitress brought Hershel his hamburger and some French fries. The man glanced at her and said, "could you bring me a coffee sweetheart?"

"Sure thing dear." The waitress replied and was off again.

"Do you mind if I sit with you and drink my coffee, Hershel? I'm just amazed at how much you look like my friend Harold."

Hershel nodded, "I don't mind, Mr...?"

"Oh, I'm sorry, where are my manners?" The man held his hand out across the table.

"John, ahh, John, Smith. I'm pleased to meet you Hershel."

The two shook hands and the waitress returned with John's coffee. He then proceeded to talk for ten minutes about his job with a shoe company and how he was on his way to close a big deal in Oklahoma City.

"Yeah, this would have been a huge contract for me. It would have meant a great Christmas for my wife and three kids. But... I guess it's going to fall through."

Hershel was chewing his food and listening with interest. He swallowed and asked, "why do you say that, John?"

John looked at him with sadness, "well, my car conked out on me. I just don't think I'll make it in time to close the deal. I'm trying my best to get there in time but I'm losing hope now. It's going to be a tight Christmas if I lose this deal. I may even lose my job."

John took another sip of his coffee and glanced at Hershel over the rim of the cup.

Hershel thought for a few seconds. Then, still holding a French fry in his hand he asked, "is Oklahoma City on highway 66?"

John perked up a little. "Yes, it's west of here, and 66 runs right through it."

"I'm going west. I could give you a ride if you want." Hershel then put the French fry in his mouth.

"Oh, my.... oh, could you do that, would you, Hershel? I would really owe you, Buddy. My goodness someone upstairs must be looking out for me. That would be so great. I could help you with gas."

The waitress brought the two tickets as John was saying this. John immediately took both.

"Your meal is on me, Hershel. You just don't know what this means to me."

"Well, it's alright John. I would hate for you to miss the meeting and have a terrible Christmas. I'm going that way anyhow." Hershel then finished off his soda as John went to pay for the meal and coffee.

When the two walked out to the Lincoln, John whistled out loud. "Wow, this is a beauty. You must be doing well. I love these Lincolns, they're beautiful cars." John then put his suitcase in the back seat.

After Hershel got in, he immediately reached over and moved his grandmother's ashes to the middle of the seat. Then John got into the front passenger seat.

"So, what do you do, Hershel? I don't think you're in the shoe business if you're driving a car like this."

As Hershel moved the Lincoln back onto the road, John put his arm on the open window and Hershel replied.

"This was my grandmother's car. She gave it to me after she passed away. I don't really do anything. I was taking care of her. But now I'm just taking her to California."

John's face twisted a bit when Hershel said this. he glanced in the back seat and then back to Hershel.

"What do you mean, you're taking her to California? I thought you said she passed away?"

"Yes, well I'm taking her ashes to California." Hershel nodded to the case sitting between them.

John looked at the case and his face again twisted a little. He recovered quickly and chuckled a bit. "Oh, I see. Well, that's real nice of you, Hershel. So, she just gave you the car?"

"Uhm, well she gave me some money too. But she gave most of her stuff to my brother. I guess she figured he had a family and needed it more than I did."

"Ahh, I see, yeah having a family costs more." John then turned and watched the scenery go by for a while.

After about an hour, Hershel pulled the wallet from his back pocket. He reached over and put it in the glove box. "Pardon me, John. This hurts my... hip after a while."

"No, it's alright. I understand, I'm the same way. That's where I generally keep mine as well." After John said this the two again watched the scenery.

Soon they passed a sign indicating they were coming into the state of Kansas.

"You ever been to Kansas, Hershel?"

"I don't think I've ever been out of Missouri." He replied.

John nodded and smiled. "Well we won't be in Kansas for long. This is just the corner of the state. We'll be coming to Oklahoma soon."

Sure enough, a ways down the road they passed the Oklahoma state sign. Later, they stopped for a quick meal to go. After this, the houses became fewer and father between as they continued west.

24

Hershel eventually began searching around nervously. "I sure need to find a restroom," he finally said aloud.

"Just stop at one of these big tree's."

Hershel glanced at John. "No, I need a real restroom."

"Ohhh," John said. "Well, we may have some trouble finding one around here." He then appeared to think of something. "I may know where one is. It's a little crude, but it may work in a pinch."

Hershel glanced at John with a look of pain in his eyes. "How far is it?"

"Oh, just a few more miles." John replied with a smile.

As the sun began to set, John pointed at an abandon gas station on the road side. Hershel pulled up beside two antique pumps.

"This place is closed." Hershel said as he looked over the boarded up and derelict store building from the window.

"Yes, but there's an outhouse in the back. I've had to use it myself several times. Like I said Hershel, it's a bit crude, but in an emergency it'll do."

The word emergency seemed to bring the urgency for a bathroom back to Hershel and he grimaced a bit in pain.

"Does it have... you know, paper?" Hershel asked, still seeming a little reluctant.

"Oh...." John looked around. He then reached into a paper bag and pulled out some napkins.

"Here you go. I didn't use my napkins from dinner. You're welcome to them."

Hershel took them. He turned the car off and pulled the keys out of the ignition. He then got out and shut the door.

John got out of the car and as Hershel was about the go around the building John called out. "Hey, Hershel."

Hershel stopped and turned around.

"Do mind if I put my bag in the trunk? I might take a little nap in the back seat later, if it's alright with you." As John said this he opened the back door on the car and pulled his suitcase out.

"Yeah, okay..." Hershel said, and reaching into his pocket pulled the keys out. He hurriedly walked back over to John and handed them to him. Then he moved quickly towards the outhouse again.

John took the keys and opened up the trunk. He moved one of Hershel's suitcases to the side. He then pulled the footstool and box of family pictures out. He sat them on the ground behind the car and put his suitcase in the empty spot. He chuckled as he shut the trunk lid.

"Way too easy," he said to himself as he got into the drivers seat of the Lincoln. He started the car and pulled away from the old pumps. He then stopped. Opening the door, he sat Ethel's ashes outside on the ground. Then John drove away in the Lincoln.

A few minutes later, Hershel walked around the abandon store to find the car gone. He jogged over to the footstool and pictures on the ground.

"Hey....what....hey?" Expressing fright, Hershel jogged down the road a little ways. He then turned and jogged the other way. He stood in the middle of the highway as dusk was overtaking the day.

With his head hanging he started walking back towards the store, then spotted the case with his grandmother's ashes. He ran to it and picked it up. He laughed a little and almost hugged the case.

Hershel then picked up the footstool and pictures and moved over to the small overhang of the old store. He sat underneath it and looked out at the road, wondering what to do.

As dusk turned to night, he sat holding the case and watching the occasional car or truck go by.

Chapter Three: Riding with Liz Taylor

Hershel slept on the hard ground under the store overhang. He awoke the next morning as the sun was rising.

Stretching his sore body, he walked around a bit to see if there were any houses around. Nothing could be seen in either direction, or down the road towards the west.

Again he sat down under the weathered overhang of the old store. Hours began to pass and he became hungry, but he still didn't leave the shade of the derelict building.

Around noon, a car dove into the old driveway of the gas station and slid to a stop. Hershel sat up.

The passenger door opened and a young woman jumped out and then slammed the door of the car, which immediately took off with tires spinning.

"Hey, what about my bag??" The young woman shouted to the car, which was already on the highway. It traveled another half-block, and then stopped. Out the window came a suitcase, landing in the middle of the road. The car then sped away with tires squealing.

"You Pig!!" The young woman shouted to the now distant car.

Hershel sat watching this with interest. The woman put her hand up to her forehead and then growled out again in anger. She stomped her feet. Then she began walking towards her suitcase.

As she got to the road, a large truck came speeding by. The horn honked long and loud. It ran over the suitcase and clothes went flying all over the highway. The truck barely slowed down.

"Aghhhhh!!" the woman shouted out again in anger. "I can't believe it! You're a pig too!" She yelled to the truck, which was almost out of sight.

Hershel stood up. The woman again began to make her way to the mess of clothing on the road.

She looked to be around twenty-five years old. She wore her light brown hair back in a high pony tail with a white tie back. Her plaid pants were rather tight fitting and came up to her calves. She also wore a white, short sleeve, turtle neck top and a small vest that matched the Capri pants. Altogether, she was fairly attractive and obviously had a sense of fashion.

As Hershel walked towards her, he could hear her mumbling to herself, under her breath. He followed behind at a distance until she reached her clothing, which had by now been overrun by another passing car.

She turned towards Hershel as she checked for oncoming traffic. When she saw him behind her she almost screamed.

"Ahhhg, who are you? Get away from me! I've got a knife!"

Hershel moved back a few steps. "I'm Hershel Lawson, Ms. I just thought you might need some help."

"Does it look like I need help? Get away from me, now!"

Hershel turned and walked slowly back to the abandoned station. He again sat under the small overhang and watched as the young woman gathered her clothing together, while avoiding oncoming traffic.

Eventually, she walked to the station with the wrecked baggage in her arms. She stood for a few seconds examining the old store. She turned and looked at the dysfunctional pumps. As she did so, a piece of clothing fell from her arms. A dusty breeze moved past them; she again turned back to the store with a puzzled expression on her face.

Hershel said nothing, but sat in the shade of the overhang and watched her curiously.

"Where is everyone?" She finally asked, as if people would start arriving at any moment.

Hershel glanced around. "I'm the only one here, Ms. Who are you talking about?"

She moved to the side of the building and looked towards the back. Several more pieces of clothing fell from her arms. "I can not believe this... Can this day get any worse?"

The young woman then walked back towards Hershel. After a few more seconds under the mid-day sun, she dropped all of the stuff in her arms. Letting out another anger filled growl, she stomped over to the opposite side of Hershel and sitting under the old overhang, put her face in her hands.

After seeming to cry for a few moments, the young woman turned to see what Hershel was doing. He simply sat watching her.

"I just want you to know, I really do have a knife." She then stared at him suspiciously.

"Oh, alright, that should come in handy."

When Hershel said this the young woman turned towards him a little more. She appeared frightened now.

"What do you mean, 'that should come in handy'? Who are you and what are you doing here?"

Before Hershel could reply the woman continued.

"And why were you sneaking up on me? I'm telling you, I do have a knife and I'm not afraid to use it!"

The young woman stood up and began to gather her things up from the ground.

"I just meant if you need to cut something, it'll be good to have a knife." Hershel replied.

"Cut what? What are you talking about? And what is this place? Why are you here at this place and no one else is here?" Again the young woman put a hand to her face and wiped the moisture from her eyes.

"Would you please tell me what's going on here?"

Hershel nodded. "Alright, I'll try. My name is Hershel Lawson. I was on my way to California. I stopped here to use the outhouse around back and a man by the name of John Smith took my car. I'm kind of stuck here, I guess. I'm thinking now that he planned on taking my car all along. I was trying to help him out by giving him a ride."

The young woman's face became relaxed some. Hershel continued.

"I wasn't trying to sneak up on you earlier. I thought you might need some help."

The young woman sat back down with her stuff. Hershel continued.

"I said it was good that you had a knife because you seem to be stuck here too. Maybe you will need to cut something."

She looked at him and shook her head a little.

"I'm not stuck here! You can stay here the rest of your life if you want. But, I'm leaving."

"Oh, is your friend coming back then?"

The young woman glanced back at Hershel with a strange expression on her face, but continued to fold her clothing and place it into a blouse. She then tied the open areas and two sleeves together, in order to fashion a makeshift bag.

"My friend? Oh, you mean the pig I was riding with? He was no friend. He said he would take me to Albuquerque. He didn't say anything about it costing me."

"How much was he trying to charge you?" Hershel asked.

She continued to work her belongings into the makeshift baggage, but replied.

"Oh he wasn't trying to charge me money. He wanted me to..." She stopped and glanced over at Hershel. Then she looked back at her task with the clothing and continued in a softer voice.

"Well, he wanted me to, do something that wasn't very nice at all. The pig. Men are such pigs."

Hershel thought about this. Then he commented, "I suspect women can be too though, right?"

The young woman finished packing her things, but again glanced over to Hershel, " yeah, probably so, but in different ways."

She then stood up and started walking towards the highway.

Hershel stood up, picked up the footstool with one arm and the box of pictures with his grandmother's ashes in it with the other. He then began to follow her.

The young woman glanced back as she reached the edge of the road.

"Why are you following me? Get away from me!"

Hershel stopped.

"I'm ahh, actually I'm going this way too. I thought maybe we could travel together."

The woman adjusted her blouse bag and started walking west. She turned and put out her thumb as a car came close and then zoomed past with a billowing of dust and hot air.

"I said get away from me, I don't want to travel with anyone!" She then walked faster in an effort to gain some distance from Hershel.

"Well, it might be helpful if we traveled together. I mean, we could help each other." Hershel said, hanging back a bit but still following behind.

The young woman stopped and turned to him.

"Do you not understand English? I said, I don't want to travel with anyone! Give me one good reason why I would want to travel with anyone, especially you?" She then turned and again started walking west.

Hershel started walking again as well, and after a few seconds replied, "Well, I'm not a pig, for one thing."

The young woman stopped, but didn't turn around. She expelled a breath of air, then gritted her teeth. She growled in frustration, but turned to Hershel.

For several seconds she simply stared at him. Finally she asked.

"Do you have any money?"

"Uhm, well, I did have almost seven hundred dollars, but John took that as well."

The woman threw her hands into the air, turned and started walking again.

"Get away from me!" She shouted.

Hershel followed again, then remembered something.

"Oh, wait I do have some money." He reached down and pulled the twenty-five dollars from his sock.

The young woman stopped and seeming very irritated turned around.

"Oh, now you have some money? Did the money fairy just visit you?"

"Well, no, I just remembered my sock money. I had some money in my sock for emergencies."

The woman walked slowly back towards Hershel.

"So, how do I know you're not a pig as well?" She asked.

He thought about this, then replied, "I guess you don't. But you don't know about the next person that gives you a ride either. They may be a pig just like the other guy."

Her face twisted slightly.

"How much money do you have?"

"Twenty-five dollars."

"Alright, here's the deal. You give me five dollars and you can travel with me to the next town. That's it, then you're on your own, got it?"

Hershel considered it briefly. Then he handed her the five dollar bill. She took it and immediately started walking west again, with Hershel following behind; constantly struggling with his odd assortment of items.

After walking a half mile down the highway, he spotted something, then quickly moved to the other side of the highway and picked up a ragged object from the road.

"What's that?" She asked as he fumbled with the item and the footstool. He then sat the stool down beside the road so he could examine the find.

"It's my wallet." Hershel said as he opened the battered leather billfold.

"No money though. John must have took the money and tossed the wallet out the window."

The woman examined Hershel as a car raced by them. The wind blew her hair about as she studied him, seeming a bit puzzled.

"So, good old John really took you to the cleaners huh?"

Hershel put the wallet in his pocket. "I suppose so. I was just trying to help him."

"Yeah, well, people are pigs. You can't trust anyone."

She sat her makeshift bag down. Hershel did likewise. Soon, another car came zooming by and Sally held her thumb out. The car never slowed down..

After several more vehicles passed by, an old pickup slowed and stopped.

"Come on!"

She quickly picked up her stuff and soon the two were jogging towards the old truck. When they reached it, an elderly man that appeared to be a farmer stuck his head out the window and looked back.

"I'm going as far as Vinita, if that will help you two."

"That'll help a lot, thanks!" The young woman said.

"Jump in the back then." The old farmer replied.

Once they were in, the old pickup got back on the road with a puff of smoke from the exhaust and a slight grinding of the gears.

As they rumbled along, Hershel took a better look at the woman. She noticed this and immediately barked out, "what are you looking at?"

Hershel smiled a little, "I just wondered why you was going to Albuquerque."

"It's none of your business."

"Okay, well, could I ask your name at least?"

She stared at him as the old pick-up bumped along. Exhaust fumes and a bit of dust danced around them as she appeared to consider his request. Finally she replied.

"Elizabeth Taylor, but you can call me Liz for short." She then gave him a quirky smile and turned to watch the scenery pass by.

"Well, thanks and it's nice to meet you, Liz."

The young woman didn't respond.

As the sun was settling on the horizon they pulled into the small town of Vinita. The young woman leaned over and talked with the farmer.

"Is there a hotel here?"

"The Clark motel is a few blocks down the road. You want me to drop you off there?"

"That would be great, thank you." She then leaned back into the pickup as the evening was turning to night.

At the motel they climbed out of the pickup and it drove on down the road.

"Well, thanks Liz." Hershel held his hand out and she rather reluctantly shook it.

"Yeah, whatever." She looked back at the motel, then again to Hershel. "So what are you going to do now?"

He looked around. "I think I'll try to find something to eat. I've not eaten since yesterday."

The woman's face winced a bit. "You should probably do that then."

As she turned and went into the motel office, Hershel examined his surroundings. Spotting a cafe down the road he went and got a cheese sandwich with water.

The following morning, the young woman came out of her room. As she walked down the sidewalk, she spotted Hershel sitting on a bench.

"So, did you sleep there last night?" She asked.

He looked up at her. "I don't know that I would call it sleeping, but yeah, I stayed here all night."

The woman's mouth twisted a bit.

"Did you find some place to eat?"

"Yeah, there's a cafe down the street a ways."

"I'm going to get some coffee, you want some?" She asked.

"That sounds good." He stood up and gathering his jumble of stuff, proceeded to follow her.

Once inside the cafe, the woman ordered toast and coffee. Hershel did the same thing.

Soon they were eating the toast and drinking the coffee.

"You see, the coffee is ten cents. Then you put the creamer and sugar in. Plus, the waitress refills the coffee when your cup gets low.

The toast is thirty-five cents, then you add the butter and jelly, and well you got a fairly decent meal for less than half a dollar."

Hershel smiled at her strategy. "That's real clever, Liz."

The young woman's smile fell from her face. She studied Hershel a few more seconds. After taking a drink of coffee she continued.

"Listen, if you promise there will be no funny stuff, maybe we can travel together for a while. But you better not try anything." Her face twisted a little as if unsure about what she was saying.

"Funny stuff like what?"

She nodded her head and replied, "yeah, that's right. Just you keep it that way, got it?"

"So, why are you headed west?" She asked, then took another bite of her toast and looked at him with interest.

"I've got to take my grandmother there, it was her last wish, for me to take her to a cemetery in Los Angeles."

"Your grandmother?" Her eyes opened a little wider.

Hershel pointed to the case inside the box of pictures, which was in the booth seat next to him. She stopped chewing her bite and pointed at it as well.

"You're telling me, I've been traveling with a dead person?"

"Well, it's just her ashes. She wanted me to take them to a special place in California. It was why she gave me her car."

The woman studied Hershel and the case for several seconds. She took another bite as a Jukebox in the corner of the cafe started playing a lively tune.

"And you say she give you some money too?"

Hershel looked down at his last few bites of toast. "Yeah, she did. Like I said, I lost the money when I lost the car."

The young woman again studied the man in the booth across from her. "I don't know how she expected you to make it to California. You're way too trusting Hershel. You got to realize there are a lot of bad people in this world."

Hershel glanced up at her. "You mean like the 'pig' that said he was going to take you to Albuquerque?"

"Exactly," she said with enthusiasm.

"Yeah, I guess so. I'm glad I can travel with you for a ways, Liz."

"Alright, stop it already, Mr. comedian."

"Stop what?" He asked.

"Stop calling me Liz."

Hershel expressed confusion, "so what should I call you then?"

"My name is Sally."

Hershel stared at her for a few seconds. Then he said with some reservation, "Sally... Taylor?"

Sally's face tightened up and she said, "If you start trying to be funny, you're on your own Mister! You got it?"

Hershel, sat back a bit. "No, I'm not going to be funny at all. Sally it is then. Just Sally, will that be alright?"

She glanced at him with suspicion again. "Yeah, well you'd better be on your best behavior, or this won't last long."

After they finished breakfast the two went back to the sidewalk.

Sally watched as Hershel fumbled with his belongings.

"Do you really need that stool?"

He glanced down at the small footstool.

"It belonged to my grandmother. I would really like to keep it."

Sally frowned and looked at the battered cardboard box with pictures inside.

"What are those?"

"They're pictures. They belonged to my grandmother too."

Sally expelled a breath of frustration. She walked over to the box and thumbed through the framed pictures.

"You've got to lighten your load. We can't get rides very easily if you're carrying everything but a kitchen sink."

She then began to take the pictures out of the frames. Hershel started to object, but she raised her hand in a manner that stopped him in mid sentence.

Soon she had all the pictures out of their frames. She placed them together and tearing the cardboard box, made a makeshift folder.

Sally then pulled a blouse from her clothes. It had been ripped up from being run over on the road. She tore strips from it and tied the cardboard folder together. She then tied on a strip that enabled him to hang the entire thing over his shoulder. She handed it to him and he examined it, appearing quiet impressed.

Again she tore several more strips from the blouse and soon had a carrying strap hooked up to the footstool as well.

"There, easier to mange and looks less... bulky. Like I said, we've got to travel light, or we won't be getting many rides."

Hershel nodded as he slung the strap of the footstool over his other shoulder and then picked up the case with his grandmother's ashes.

With their makeshift luggage, the two walked down the street from the cafe. Hershel passed a trash can and tossed the remainder of the cardboard box along with the picture frames into it.

By nine o'clock the two were walking west, out of Vinita, with their thumbs in the air.

An hour later they were once again riding in the back of a dated pickup truck. Hershel watched Sally. She again noticed this.

"What...? Why do you keep looking at me?"

Hershel turned away. "I'm sorry. I just wondered why you was traveling."

Sally replied quickly, "I already told you, it's none of your business!"

"Alright, I'm sorry, Sally." He then looked back as the long stretch of highway slipped by.

Sally turned away as well. Then after a few minutes she glanced at Hershel. The anger on her face melted away. She looked down at the makeshift baggage between her legs.

"I'm going to California to be an actress, alright? So, go ahead and laugh if you want, but I don't care. My parents already told me it's impossible, and ever one else did as well. My sister, her husband and everyone in that blasted little one horse town I left has already told me. So what does it matter if you tell me too. But I'm going to make it. I know I can, so I don't care what you or anyone else has to say about it."

She never looked at Hershel while saying this and afterwards turned away from him as if preparing for his comment.

Hershel's face expressed concern as the warm breeze blew their hair about.

"I don't think it's impossible, Sally. I think you can be an actress if you want to be."

Sally turned to him. At first she seemed happy that he said this. Then her face became twisted again.

"What are you up to? I told you, no funny stuff. I swear, Hershel, you better quit messing around."

"What... I'm not up to anything, Sally."

"You think I'm stupid?"

"No, Sally I said I thought you can do it if you want."

She gave him a sour look.

"You think I don't know what you're up to but I do. I'm not stupid. I'm watching you. You may think you're fooling me but you're not."

Sally then scooted away from him and again watched the scenery going by.

Hershel grimaced from the harsh words. He then slumped down a little and for the next twenty miles neither said anything.

Later, as they again stood on the side of the highway, Hershel attempted some conversation.

"Sally, are you mad at me?"

The young woman growled as another car passed by them.

"Hershel, I know about men like you, alright. You say the things a woman wants to hear and act all innocent and polite. But I know what you're trying to get and once you get what you want.... then you're gone. I'm not stupid, okay?"

Hershel considered this a few seconds. "What is it I'm trying to get?"

Sally growled again, "ahhhhgggg...... That's what I'm talking about." she pointed her finger at him. "You'd better stop it." She then started walking away from him.

A semi-truck stopped ahead of her and she started jogging towards it. Hershel also jogged behind her. Once inside, they found a man of around fifty. He seemed friendly, especially to Sally.

For the next few hours the truck driver and Sally talked about almost everything under the sun. She laughed at his jokes and before they knew it, they had gone through Tulsa and were pulling into Sapulpa.

"I'm heading south up here a ways, Sweetheart."

The truck driver had, for many miles, been calling Sally a variety of affectionate names. Sally had neglected to discourage him after the first one and from that point on the truck driver ventured over almost every pet name Hershel had ever heard, and a few he hadn't.

"Thank you, Hank. We're going west, but we really do appreciate the ride." The truck came to a stop at an intersection, as the sun was hitting the horizon. Sally and Hershel crawled out of the cab with their makeshift baggage.

Later, they bought an order of French fries at a cafe and continued walking through town while eating them.

"So, are you going to get a room?" Hershel asked as the street lights were coming on.

"A room costs six dollars. If I keep getting a room I'll run out of money." Sally spoke in a frustrated tone and then stuck another French fry in her mouth.

"I was just asking." Hershel followed a few feet behind her. "Why are you so nice to a guy like Hank and not so nice to me?"

Sally stopped. She turned and looked at Hershel as a car whizzed past them.

"Because I know what guys like Hank are after and they ain't gonna get it. You're too nice, Hershel. You're always so polite and saying things that I like to hear. I don't like that."

She then continued to walk alongside the street.

"So, you want me to not be nice?" He asked as he tried to catch up with her.

"You see, right there...." She turned and faced him again. "That's what I'm talking about. If I say I don't want you to be nice, then I'm the bad girl right? But if I say I want you to be nice then it means I'm giving in to you. I'm not easy like that."

She turned again and continued while Hershel stood in confusion. He scratched the side of his head and then stuck another French fry in his mouth.

He followed behind her until they came to a bus station. She sat her baggage on a bench outside the building. Inside there was a small coffee shop and a few patrons on stools.

"I'm staying here tonight." She sat on the bench, seeming to still be upset.

"Alright," Hershel said and went to the bench beside the one she sat on. He put his baggage down and sat, quietly glancing over to Sally from time to time.

They slept restlessly on the hard benches as an occasional bus would pull through with much noise and exhaust fumes.

When dawn began to break, Sally nudged Hershel. "Come on, let's get some coffee."

They sat in the small shop sipping coffee and eating toast.

"Hershel, I didn't mean to get so upset yesterday. That's all I'm going to say, okay?" She then looked at him from over the rim of her coffee cup.

"Okay, and I'm sorry if I said something wrong to you."

"I said, that was all I'm going to say about it. Don't start again." She then stared at him a few seconds, seeming almost ready to pounce on him.

Hershel nodded sheepishly and picked up his coffee.

After cleaning up some in the bus station restrooms, they stopped by a store to buy some crackers and a few other inexpensive food and drink items, then once again got on the highway.

40

Chapter Four: A Romp At Ms. Rose's House

As they reached the outskirts of Sapulpa, a large Cadillac stopped. It was a two tone green, Coupe Deville. Sally and Hershel jogged up to the car.

Hershel opened the door for Sally and a cloud of cigarette smoke billowed out.

"Set your stuff in the back seat there. You two can ride up here with me, there's plenty of room."

As Hershel sat their baggage in the back, he glanced at the woman driving. She was around forty-five or so and had brown hair, which was in a hairdo that almost touched the top of the car inside. She was somewhat pretty for her age, but the cigarette hanging from her mouth was not helping matters.

Sally slid into the front seat and Hershel sat beside her. Soon the large car was back on the highway headed west.

"Rose Robins," the woman said as she expelled a cloud of cigarette smoke across the two passengers.

Sally smiled and seemed to be trying her best not to cough. Then she braced up and replied, "I'm Sally and this is Hershel."

Ashes dropped onto Rose's lap and she dusted them off. "I'm pleased to meet you. So, where are you two headed?"

"Amarillo," Sally replied before Hershel could say anything.

"Oh my, well I can take you to this side of Oklahoma City, but that's as far as I'm going." Rose then expelled another drag of smoke from her nose and mouth.

"Thank you, Rose, that will help a lot." Sally again spoke for the two of them.

As they rode along, Rose lit one cigarette from another and spoke about her modeling career when she was younger. This seemed to amount to some photos in various regional magazines, combined with a variety of clothes modeling jobs for companies in Oklahoma City.

The Cadillac slowed as she spoke and Hershel thought they must be traveling a mere forty miles per hour at times, though he couldn't see the speedometer from his vantage point.

Eventually, they stopped to eat and Sally ordered two coffees and a hamburger, which she cut in two for her and Hershel. Rose watched this curiously but then lit a cigarette up and proceeded to eat and smoke at the same time.

As the afternoon was moving closer to evening, Rose pulled the large Cadillac into a long driveway of a large two story mansion. The elaborately ornate house sat in the middle of nowhere as there was nothing else around. In the distance some tall buildings could be seen and the two travelers imagined this must be Oklahoma City.

"Welcome to the house of Rose. We love having guests. It's too late to be traveling, won't you two stay the night?" Rose smiled without a cigarette in her mouth and Hershel noticed her teeth were in a good condition, other than being stained yellow from the smoke.

Sally glanced at Hershel and Hershel sort of shrugged his shoulders.

"Well, it is kind of late to be on the road. Are you sure it won't be any trouble, Rose?" As Sally said this, Rose lit another cigarette up and a cloud of smoke floated once again through the front seat of the Cadillac.

"No trouble at all dear. We have guests here all the time, and we love to entertain. You two stay a while and rest up. Amarillo can wait."

A man stepped up to the car and opened the door for Rose. Hershel then opened his door and he and Sally got out.

"Arnold, these young folks will be staying with us for a while. Please have their baggage brought in after you park the car."

"Yes, Ms. Rose."

Arnold got into the Cadillac as Hershel was attempting to get the baggage out of the back seat.

"Leave those things for Arnold, Hon. It'll give him something to do." Rose then walked up the front steps. Hershel quickly grabbed the case with his grandmother's ashes. He and Sally then followed rather cautiously behind Rose.

As they moved through the front of the house, music could be heard in a room to their right. The laughter of a woman was heard in another direction. A maid came to them and bowed slightly to Rose."

"I've started running your bath, Ms. Rose."

"Thank you Lydia. Please take these two young people to a guest room, they'll be staying with us for a while. They've been traveling and need to rest up a bit. Let Arnold know where to deliver their baggage."

Lydia bowed again. "Yes, Ms. Rose."

She then motioned to Sally and Hershel. "Follow me please."

As they walked up the stairs, Lydia turned back to them, "will you be needing one room or two?"

Without hesitation, Hershel and Sally both replied in unison, "two."

Lydia took them both to very nice rooms. Hershel carefully placed his grandmothers' ashes on a chest of drawers, then proceeded to get settled in. Sally was soon soaking in a warm bath and resisted getting out until after the water had cooled down.

A few hours later, a knock on Hershel's door brought him to his feet. Opening the door, he found Sally standing outside, but looking towards the stairs.

Hershel realized she was listing to music and the sound of many voices downstairs.

"What do you think is going on down there?" Sally asked.

After stepping into the hallway, Hershel listened for a few seconds. There was laughter amongst the voices and music being played on a piano. Then a woman sang a verse of the song being played. She sang loudly and everyone laughed when she finished the verse. Hershel finally replied.

"Sounds like a family gathering. We should probably stay up here."

Sally nodded, "yeah, I think so. Do you have any of those crackers left?"

"Yeah, I was thinking about those as well."

Hershel gave her some of the snacks they had bought and then sat in the room eating crackers and drinking tap water as the sounds downstairs increased throughout the night. Finally around ten o'clock, he went to bed.

The next morning, Hershel was woken by another knock on the door. He cracked the door open and once again found Sally outside.

"Come on, get dressed. I want to go down stairs."

"I can't. I washed my 'one' set of clothes last night and I don't think they're dry yet."

Sally expressed aggravation at this.

"Can't you put them on a little damp? I don't want to go downstairs by myself. And, I'm starving, ain't you?"

Hershel thought for a few seconds as he held the door open to a small crack. "Yeah, alright, just a minute," he replied and shut the door.

A few moments later, the two crept downstairs to find Lydia and several other maids cleaning a large parlor. They moved on until coming to a kitchen. Here they found several attractive young women dressed in lingerie, standing by a counter and drinking coffee.

Hershel tried to turn away, but before he could do anything, one of the women spoke.

"Well, hello there handsome."

Hershel and Sally were both bewildered by the sight and the greeting. Hershel looked down at the floor.

"I'm sorry, we were just looking around. I'm Sally and this is Hershel, we're guests of Ms. Rose," Sally spoke for both of them as Hershel appeared too embarrassed to say anything.

The two women seemed to notice Sally after she said this, but they moved over to Hershel, still holding their coffee cups in hand.

"Oh, is this your husband then?" One of the women asked.

"Him? No he's not my husband!" Sally quickly replied.

The women now began to look Hershel over. "Is he your boyfriend?" The other woman asked.

"No, he's nothing to me.. Well, a friend maybe, I guess, but not a boyfriend." Sally again seemed rather upset that the women asked such a thing.

"Well, in that case, my name is Polly and this is Franchesca." One of the young women said to Hershel.

"Uhmm, hello." Hershel replied, meekly. He continued to stare at the floor as the two women came even closer.

Polly giggled, "Hershel, are you embarrassed? Have you never seen a woman in her sleeping clothes before?"

Sally stepped back as Polly and Franchesca paid no more attention to her.

Hershel began to blush, "uhm, no. I've never seen a woman in her sleeping clothes before. I'm sorry, I should leave." He began to back towards the door.

"Nonsense, Hershel, you stay right here and have some coffee with us." Franchesca replied, and taking Hershel by the arm pulled him over to a table as the two women giggled.

Soon, Hershel was drinking coffee and laughing with the two women. Sally stood watching for a few minutes and then went to pour herself a cup of coffee.

"So, where are you from, Hershel?" Polly smiled after asking this and then took a sip of her coffee.

"St. Louis" He replied.

"St. Louis! Oh I've always wanted to go there!" Franchesca then pushed Hershel's arm lightly and giggled.

Sally moved over to a smaller table. She sat down and shook her head. Soon a maid came in with a tray of food. As the maid began to distribute plates, more young women came into the large kitchen area and also began to make a fuss over Hershel.

As Sally ate breakfast, she glanced over at Hershel as he blushed and smiled. It was obvious he'd never had this much attention in his life, much less from a host of attractive young women, in their "sleeping clothes".

After breakfast, Hershel was ushered out back to the swimming pool. Sally went to her room, but eventually made her way to the pool as well.

She found Hershel sitting in a lounge chair. He was wearing a pair of ladies sunglasses, a short sleeve dress shirt and swimming trunks. His pale white legs almost beamed in the sunlight. Yet the young women gathered around him as if he were a famous singer or actor.

Sally took a seat and watched as the ladies came and went in their rather tiny swimming suits. Eventually, there came a time when Hershel had no women around him. Sally went over to him as he reclined under the shade of a large umbrella.

"Hershel, what are you doing? And where did you get those clothes?"

He looked up at her thru the white, horn rimmed sunglasses.

"What are you talking about? I'm just sitting here. And, Polly gave me the clothes. She said men leave clothes here all the time, and don't ever come back for them."

Sally grunted, "I don't doubt that, but, you shouldn't be getting so friendly with all these women. They're all... well, you know."

Hershel looked across the pool at one of the young women as she climbed out of the water. He then glanced back up to Sally.

"They're what, Sally?"

Again Sally grunted with frustration. "Hershel... don't you know anything? They, well, they're all, tainted women."

"That's not a very nice thing to say, Sally. Are you jealous because they're talking to me?"

Sally grimaced as the young woman from across the pool approached.

"No I'm not jealous, Hershel. You're just an idiot!" She then stormed away as the woman toweled herself off and sat down beside Hershel.

Not long after this, Ms. Rose came out to the pool. She was smoking her seemingly endless cigarette and carrying what looked to be a mixed drink.

As she stood in front of the pool, Hershel examined the woman through the borrowed sunglasses. She wore a one piece bathing suit and a delicate, see through, lace robe over it. A broad brimmed, white hat rested on her head. It was a southern styled hat and Hershel had seen many women in St. Louis wearing similar ones.

As he examined Ms. Rose, she turned and noticed him laying back in the lounge chair.

"Well, hello there, Henry. Are you enjoying the day?" She then took another drag from her cigarette and expelled the smoke in a feminine manner.

"Uhm, yes Ms. Rose, I am. And, it's actually Hershel."

"Well that's good, we always strive to please our male guests. So, where is that petite little gal friend of yours? Is she enjoying her stay as well? I might just offer her a job, she would be quite a looker, if dolled up some."

"I think she's doing well, Ms. Rose." Hershel stood up. "And, if there's anything I can do around here to help, I would be happy to do so. You've been very kind to let us stay here awhile."

Ms. Rose stepped back and then looked Hershel over from head to toe. She smiled and seemed to have a little trouble standing in one spot.

"Well, I might just take you up on that, Harry. I could use a good strong, maintenance man..." She winked at him and then took another drink.

"That would be great, Ms. Rose. Just whatever you need me to do."

Ms. Rose moaned and smiled with glee. The young woman that had sat down beside Hershel giggled rather loudly.

"Well, big boy. For now, you can just... oh, clean the pool or something. And, be sure to flex those muscles while you're at it." She squinted her nose and smiled slyly, then took another drag from her cigarette and staggered back towards the house. Again the young woman in the lounge chair giggled and smiled at Hershel.

"Alright, Ms. Rose, I'll do that. And thank you!" Hershel replied in a loud voice as Ms. Rose entered the back door.

The following day, Sally again went to the pool. There stood Hershel with a net attached to a long pole. He was carefully capturing a few leaves and pulling them from the otherwise clean water.

Sally watched him for a few seconds and noticed he wore the swimming trunks from the previous day, but a different dress shirt, and the sleeves had been cut off of this one. She expelled a breath of frustration and walked over to him.

"Hershel, what are you doing? And what happened to the sleeves on that shirt?"

Still wearing the borrowed women's sunglasses, Hershel looked at her with a puzzled expression.

"I'm cleaning the pool, Sally, why would you ask such a thing?"

Sally glanced to the other side of the pool and quickly pointed to Polly and another young woman reclining in lounge chairs and watching Hershel from behind stylish sunglasses.

"You're putting on a show, Hershel. That's what your doing. I'm guessing one of those ladies cut off the sleeves of that shirt before giving it to you?"

"Well, Polly cut them off, and then gave the shirt to me, along with two pair of pants. She said the shirt would be cooler this way and I could catch a breeze."

Again Sally expelled a breath of frustration.

"Hershel, we need to leave. If you remember, we're on our way to California."

After a few seconds of thought and some additional skimming with the net, Hershel replied.

"I'm not ready to leave, Sally. I told Ms. Rose I would help with the pool. Besides, what difference does a few days make?"

Sally grimaced, her mouth twisted in anger just before replying in a loud voice.

"I'll tell you what difference it makes, Hershel. I heard some of the ladies talking in the kitchen this morning. They say you've got virg-." Sally paused and stepped back. Then continued with a lower voice. "Well, they say you've got something written all over you.

48

And these ladies would certainly know. And I'm thinking you're becoming the subject of a challenge for them."

Hershel stood staring at her. She couldn't tell what he was thinking due to the women's sunglasses he wore. After a few seconds he replied.

"Have you been drinking, Sally? You really shouldn't drink this early in the morning. I know Ms. Rose does, but she's older than you."

"Ahhggg," Sally threw her hands up and again stormed away.

The next day Hershel was trimming the bushes around the pool when Sally came up to him.

"Hello Hershel."

"Hi Sally, are you still mad at me?"

Sally expelled a breath of air, "It's not that I'm mad. You just.." She then noticed Hershel's shirt had the sleeves cut off, again.

"Did Polly cut the sleeves off another shirt?"

Hershel glanced down at his bare arms. "I'm not sure, it was like this when she gave it to me."

Sally shook her head. "Hershel, do you know anything about women?"

Hershel stopped his trimming and again gave Sally a puzzled expression.

"Well, I like women. And I really like the women here. They're real nice, and pretty."

Sally stared at him for a few seconds. He reached up and pushed the white, ladies' sunglasses up on his nose. She suddenly realized how ridiculous and yet innocent he appeared. She chuckled under her breath.

"You're either a great actor or way too naive. Around here, either one can get you into trouble."

Hershel's head twisted as he considered her statement.

He then smiled. "You should go swimming, the pool is really great. Maybe Polly has a suit you could borrow."

Sally stared at him for several seconds before replying. "Yeah, you would like that wouldn't you? Sorry, but I'm not getting into one of those tiny things they call a swimming suit." She then glanced over to the pool. "I've got a pair of shorts though. Since you obviously like living dangerously, I may as well make the most of it."

Hershel again looked at her from behind the ladies sunglasses; seeming puzzled by her comment.

Sally changed into a pair of shorts, then laid in a reclining chair beside the pool with several other ladies to get some sun.

That evening there was more music and laughter in the parlor. Sally sat at the top of the stairs, listening and catching glimpses of the activity below. Hershel came and sat down beside her.

"Everyone seems so happy, don't they. I like it here."

Sally turned and again examined him closely.

"If you say so. But, we should be leaving soon."

Yeah, but we can stay a while longer can't we? I'm really enjoying it. And besides, Ms. Rose said she might offer you a job."

Sally appeared to almost explode when Hershel said this. She looked at him with anger in her eyes."

"I ought to slap you right here and right now!"

"What?" He asked.

"You're just a regular comedian aren't you? You stay here if you want, but I'm leaving. I'm going to California with or without you!"

"What?" He asked again.

She then stood up and stormed back to her room.

Hershel turned and watched her until she slammed the door behind her.

"She's absolutely nuts!" He then turned back to listen to the events happening downstairs. Eventually he grew sleepy and went to bed.

In the predawn light, a gunshot rang out. Hershel sat up, shocked by the sound.

As he began to climb out of bed, another gunshot rang out.

He pulled his pants on and went out the door. There, Sally and a number of the ladies along with several men stood as if also aroused by the sounds.

"What's going on?" Sally asked.

As soon as she asked this, another shot rang out and the window at the end of the hallway appeared to explode. Glass flew everywhere and women screamed.

Everyone immediately fell to the floor.

Hershel crawled closer to Sally as another shot rang out and more glass was heard shattering in another part of the house.

Sally spoke up at this point.

"Shouldn't someone call the police?"

Polly lay a few doors down from Sally and answered in a hushed voice, "We call the sheriff around these parts, Hon."

Another shot rang out and more glass shattered.

"Well, can someone call the sheriff and see if he can do something?"

Polly turned her head back and spoke to the man laying on the floor that had come from her room.

"Rodger, Hon, could you do something about this?"

Just as the man was about to answer, a woman outside shouted in a loud and angry voice, "Rodger P Clanton! I know you're in there, you two-timing skunk! You come out here and face me like a man!"

Everyone in the upstairs hallway looked to Rodger. He just shook his head in dismay.

Polly then asked him, "Did you leave a gun where Shirley could find it, Hon?"

"She stopped drinkin! Or so she said. And, I thought I had it hid good!" Rodger replied, just as another shot rang out and more glass shattered.

Rose crawled to the foot of the stairs.

"Rodger, be a dear please and go calm your wife, before she demolishes our home."

"Sorry Rose, but there's no way I'm going out there! If you hadn't noticed, she's got a shotgun!"

"Rodger, you better get out here you scum bag!" Shirley shouted and then shot out another window.

Sally crawled over to Hershel.

"This is all your fault!"

"What are you talking about, I don't know either one of them!

Sally grimaced and lowered her head as another shot rang out.

"Well, Rodger, dear, someone needs to do something, and you are the sheriff." Rose yelled up from the bottom of the stairs.

"Yes, well... she'll run out of ammunition sooner or later, Rose!" he replied.

Another shot rang out and another window shattered. The sun began to creep up over the horizon.

"Alright Rodger, but just so you know, you'll be buying me some new windows and curtains." Rose shouted.

Rodger let out a groan, "yeah, fine Rose. That'll be fine."

Then a number of shots rang out in rapid succession. Rodger crept over and cautiously peeked out the corner of a destroyed window.

"Awww, nooo." He said.

"What's wrong, Hon?" Polly asked, still laying low.

"She just shot up my car." He replied with agony. "And it was last year's model."

A car door was then heard slamming shut and tires spinning as Shirley sped away.

"Looks like it's clear. But I think I'll sleep at the office for a few days till she cools down some." Sheriff Clanton then stood all the way up and looked out the window.

Sally stood up and went straight into her room. Hershel stood up and examined the glass and broken windows. Everyone else in the hallway was doing the same when a few minutes later Sally came out of her room carrying her makeshift baggage.

"Where're you going?" Hershel asked as she moved towards the stairs.

"I'm leaving, Hershel, right now!"

"Well, wait for me!"

She stopped and stared at him with anger filled eyes. "I'll give you thirty seconds, that's it."

Hershel's eyes widened. He darted into his room, threw on one of the sleeveless shirts and gathered his things together, including the other articles of clothing that Polly had given him. Just as he was stepping out the door with his arms filled, Sally again began walking down the stairs.

On the first floor they found a similar scene of destruction as the one they had left on the second floor. Several of the ladies walked around in negligees, seeming a bit dazed. Glass lay strewn all around, but there were two servants already beginning the clean up.

In the middle of this stood Ms. Rose, also in sleeping clothes, smoking a cigarette and talking with Lydia.

"And since our dear friend Sheriff Clanton will be paying, I think we'll go with the red, crushed velvet curtains this time. I've been wanting to change them anyway."

Sally had slowed some in order to not interrupt. But as soon as Lydia nodded and said, "Yes, MS Rose," Sally moved up closer.

"We'll be leaving now, Ms. Rose. Thank you for the hospitality."

MS Rose had been staring at the shattered windows but turned to Sally and then to Hershel.

"Oh, well, must you really be leaving so soon, Henry?"

Hershel wasn't actually prepared to talk to Ms. Rose, and when Sally looked at him with even more anger in her eyes, he almost dropped everything he was struggling to hold onto.

"Uhmm, well, I uh guess we do need to go, Ms. Rose. Thank you for everything."

He then darted towards the door after Sally, who walked away as soon as Ms. Rose spoke to Hershel rather than her.

Outside, he fumbled with his belongings as he passed Rodger Clanton's shot up car. Then as he was able to put the strap of the footstool over his shoulder and get a better hold on his grandmother's ashes, he almost sprinted to catch up to Sally.

"Can you please slow down?"

She slowed and looked back at him, then took off again at the same brisk pace.

"What's wrong with you?" He almost shouted out.

This caused her to stop completely and turn back to him.

"What's wrong with me? What's wrong with me? How about, we were almost killed? How about that?" She then took off towards the highway again.

"Yeah, well we didn't get killed, Sally. And, why are you acting so mean to me?"

She stopped again.

"I told you we should leave two days ago. But no, you wanted to stay here and lay around the pool with your girlfriends. If we'd left when I said we should have, we wouldn't have been almost killed."

She then started walking again but not quite as fast.

Hershel continued to arrange his burdens and was now almost side by side with her.

"They're not my girlfriends. And how was I to know something like that would happen?"

Sally just growled at this as they came up to the highway. Hershel remained quiet and slightly behind her as they began walking along the long stretch of road.

After several miles without catching a ride, an old panel van pulled over. Soon they found themselves sitting in the back of it and amongst TV parts and tools, all of which rattled about with much noise.

Occasionally Sally glanced at Hershel or he glanced at her, but neither said anything.

For more than an hour the old TV repair van rumbled along. Then, it pulled over to the side and the repairman turned back to them, "I'm getting off the highway here. You two want out or do you want to go to Bethany with me?"

"We'll get out here, thank you." Sally replied and they climbed out the back doors to find themselves on the western edge of Oklahoma City.

They soon came to a small drug store.

"I've got to go buy something. You stay here." Sally said.

"Well, I need to look for something, I'll go in too."

"No you won't! You stay here like I said!"

Hershel studied her as she glared at him. Then he replied, "you're not my boss, Sally, I need to go in too."

She appeared to swell up. "I told you... I need to buy something. I don't want you in there when I buy... what I need to buy!"

Hershel considered this for a second. "Okay, that's fine, you need to buy something. But why do I have to stay out here?"

Sally growled a little, but then said, "because... it's... time... alright?"

"It's time?" He asked.

"Yes, so you stay out here."

"Well, can you at least tell me what's so important that I've got to stand out here in the heat, while you go inside to do your shopping?"

"I just told you!"

Hershel's face twisted slightly.

"Told me what? It's.. time? Time for you to buy something?"

"Yes! and why are you making this so difficult?"

"I'm making it difficult?"

"Yes!" She almost shouted.

"I just want you to tell me what you're going to buy. How is that so difficult?"

"You know what I'm going to buy. Why do I have to say it? So you can laugh?" She stared at him and then continued. "I know what this is about. This is about this morning isn't it? You just want to punish me for tearing you away from those women."

"Wait... what are you talking about, Sally? I thought we was talking about what you were going in to buy."

"No, we're talking about you trying to make me say... what I'm not going to say. This is about you trying to get me back isn't it?"

"I just want to know what it is your buying. And why I've got to stay out here while you buy it."

Sally's face twisted in anger. "You know good and well what I've got to buy. You just want to punish me by making me say it."

Hershel, stepped back a bit and looked at the store for a second, then back to her.

"I know what your going to buy?" He asked.

"Of course you do. You just want me to say it so you can have your revenge, but I'm not giving you the pleasure."

"Sally, if I know what you're going to buy, why does it matter if I go in the store or not?"

"Because... you might, see what kind I'm buying!"

"What kind of what?"

"Stop it, Hershel! You may think it's funny. I know men may joke about it all the time. But it's not funny and I don't appreciate you making fun of me."

"I'm making fun of you?"

"You see! Just like that! Right there!" She pointed her finger at him. "You're just having a jolly old time now aren't you? You just want me to say it so you can laugh while I'm in there buying... them."

"Them? You mean, you need more than one?"

Sally's face became red. She looked as if she was about to explode.

"Are you through making fun of me? Have you punished me enough?"

Hershel raised his hands up in dismay.

"I'm not making fun of you, Sally! You said it's 'time' for you to buy something. You won't tell me what it is, because you say I already know. But I'm suppose to stay out here so I don't see what kind your buying!"

56

She continued to glare at him, then said, "Exactly, so... why are you making this so complicated?"

Hershel expelled a long breath of frustration.

"I don't know, Sally. I really don't know. I'll stay out here while you go buy... whatever it is you need to buy."

Several minutes later she came out with a sack and two cold sodas. She quickly stashed the sack in her blouse bag.

She then handed one of the sodas to Hershel without saying a word and started walking west.

Walking behind Sally, Hershel took a sip of his drink. He watched her take a sip as well. Then a car sped by and caused a dusty breeze to blow her hair about.

She tried to pull a lose strand of the hair from her face but struggled with the soda and her tied up blouse with clothes inside.

"I'm, really sorry, Sally. Are you still mad at me?" He asked while following behind her.

The sun was easing towards the horizon as she turned to him.

"Would you just stop, Hershel."

Hershel stopped walking. "Okay."

Sally grimaced and stopped. "No, I mean stop all the 'goody two shoes crap.'" She sat her stuff on the ground and then reached up and readjusted the bothersome hairs.

"Look, you may have had all those women at Rose's place fooled and lined up to... do whatever. But you're not fooling me, alright?"

She picked her stuff back up and began walking again just as Hershel replied, "alright... I guess?"

As the sun began to sink below the horizon, Sally left the highway and began walking towards a small country church that sat a few blocks from the road.

Upon reaching the old church, she walked into the small enclosed entryway. After a brief examination of the area, she sat down in front of the double doors.

Hershel looked inside and then entered the enclosure as well.

"What are we doing here?" He asked, as Sally began placing the bundle of clothes down in a manner to use as a pillow.

"What does it look like? We're staying the night here. And you better not try anything. I still have my knife."

Hershel sat down but didn't feel comfortable. After a few seconds he said, "we're trespassing, Sally. I don't think we should stay here."

Sally had laid back on her makeshift baggage but after hearing this she sat up.

"Who owns this place, Hershel?"

He considered this for a few seconds.

"I suppose it belongs to the church."

"Alright, well isn't it a 'house of God'?" She asked.

Again he considered this as darkness settled in and he could barely make out her face.

"I suppose it is."

"Well, if God tells us to leave, then we'll leave. If not, then I figure he's alright with us staying the night here. Fair enough?"

She laid back as he considered this. Finally he replied, "I guess so," and also began making himself as comfortable as possible.

A long and uncomfortable night finally gave way to the sun breaking over the horizon.

Sally and Hershel both stretched with obvious agony from sleeping on the hard wood floor. They were relieved to find an outhouse behind the church and even happier to find it stocked with bathroom tissue.

Soon they were back on the highway, eating crackers and holding their thumbs out.

After getting a short ride of around ten miles, the two were once again hitchhiking.

"I think I'll have to get a room tonight." Sally said, almost as if talking to herself.

"Alright, I guess I'll get one too then." Hershel replied, feeling glad that she was talking again.

Sally stopped walking and turned to him.

"How much money do you have?"

"Eighteen dollars and some change." he said.

She strained in thought as another large truck passed by, blowing dust all around.

"I've got forty seven dollars and some change. A room will cost six dollars at least, which will put me at forty one dollars and you at twelve."

She let out a breath of frustration and continued. "That's not good. We're not even through Oklahoma yet. We've got to find some way to earn money."

Hershel nodded and adjusted the strap of his footstool. "Yeah, but if we work somewhere, won't we need to live somewhere too?"

Sally took a small bite of her cracker and chewed it thoughtfully.

"I'm thinking small jobs. Like... you know what they call 'odd jobs.' If we can do little jobs then maybe we can earn money without needing to stay in that area for a long time."

Sally then turned and began walking down the road again. Hershel followed her and caught up to her as she began talking again.

"Can you paint or build stuff?"

"Well, not really. I can use a push mower and hedge clippers."

Sally looked at him with a puzzled expression. She then stuck her thumb out as another car came close and then passed by.

"What kinda guy can't paint or build stuff? Didn't your Daddy teach you anything?"

Hershel frowned. "Not really. My Daddy died when a was a baby."

Sally stopped and appeared very saddened. "Oh, I'm sorry. I.. well, I'm really sorry."

"It's alright. I don't remember him at all. I only know what my grandmother told me about him. She said he was a very good man. So I'm proud of that."

They soon caught another ride that took them to the western edge of El Reno. Since it was afternoon by this time, they decided not to take a chance on going farther. They stopped at a cafe and split a hamburger, then found a small motel and each rented a room for the night.

Both eagerly cleaning up. Then washed their clothes in the sink and bathtub. Soon there were pants, shirts, blouses and underwear hanging all over each room.

The following morning, Hershel stepped over to Sally's room and knocked on the door. She somewhat reluctantly let him in.

"How much farther to California?" He asked.

Sally was sitting on the bed eating a cracker, while staring blankly into space, seemingly in deep thought. She looked at Hershel as he sat in a chair also eating crackers and watching her in anticipation of an answer.

"A lot farther. Our luck had better change soon. We're not going to make it otherwise."

Hershel thought about this.

"It's always darkest right before the dawn."

Sally smiled, though very slightly. "That sounds real good. But it won't get us any closer to California."

Later, they gathered their luggage together and waited until just before check out time to leave as neither one's clothes had completely dried.

Chapter Five: Giddy Up

As the two walked towards the outskirts of El Reno, the overcast day grew darker. Soon it began to rain. Sally and Hershel found themselves huddled under the protective awning of a service station.

"What was that, darkest before dawn thing you was talking about?" Sally asked as she gazed out into the pouring rain.

Hershel shrugged when she glanced at him.

For an hour they watched as the cars came and left the service station.

Then, a small bus that looked to be an early forties model and possibly military surplus, pulled into the service station.

Hershel noticed the drab green vehicle right away as it had a guitar painted on the side and "Tex Witherspoon" underneath it in colorful text.

"Look, it's Tex Witherspoon!" Hershel said enthusiastically. Sally was sitting on the footstool, holding the makeshift bag on her lap and reading a newspaper that she had found discarded in the ladies bathroom.

"Who's Tex Witherspoon?" She asked and stood up.

A tall man in his mid forties and dressed in cowboy attire stepped off the bus; looking around he immediately noticed Sally and Hershel. He looked at them a bit longer than Sally thought he should for just a passing glance. The man then adjusted his cowboy hat and said something to the service station attendant, who quickly began fueling the bus.

"You mean to say you've never heard of Tex Witherspoon?" Hershel asked.

"No, who is he?" Sally questioned as she watched the man walk towards the men's restroom.

"He's a singer."

"What does he sing?" She asked.

"Well, he sings country songs."

"What are some of his songs?"

Hershel strained in thought.

"You don't know any of his songs?" Sally asked.

"Not really."

"Have you ever heard of Tex Witherspoon? Or did you just read it on the side of the bus?"

Hershel expressed discomfort. "Sure, I've heard of him, I think... I mean the name sounds familiar."

"You think you've heard of him? Either you've heard of him or you haven't."

"Well, if his name sounds familiar, then it's most likely that I've heard of him."

They were so busy discussing this that both were shocked when the man suddenly spoke from behind them.

"You two looking for work?" His voice had a raspy southern drawl and both jumped a bit when he asked this.

As they turned around, Sally put her hand to her chest. "You almost scared the pee out of me, Mister!"

"I'm sorry Ma'am." He then eyed her up and down, as if sizing her up for something.

"Well," she glanced at Hershel. He looked back at her.

"We might be. But we're actually trying to get to California." She replied, seeming apprehensive and flattered both that he was giving her the extra attention.

"I'm headed west as well. But I'll be making a number of stops along the way. My assistant ran off with another singer back in Tulsa. I think you're about the same size as her and could wear the outfit." He again eyed her from top to bottom.

Sally smiled, seeming glad the singer had a purpose in sizing her figure up.

"Uhm, Hershel, what do you think?"

Tex, then looked at Hershel, "can you drive? I need someone that can drive and carry equipment."

62

"Yes Sir, I can drive." Hershel replied with a smile.

Tex looked them over again. "It don't pay much. But if you two are headed to California then it'll get you a little closer."

Now Hershel noticed that Sally was smiling as well.

"Alright, if we can get closer to California and help you some as well, that sounds good!" She replied with enthusiasm.

Tex then nodded and with a quick, "alright then," they found themselves following him to the small bus.

Sally and Hershel climbed in as Tex paid for the gas. Inside, they could see there were two bench seats in the front and two in the back. The two in the back had been turned into a bed and there was blankets strewn across it.

The seats in the middle had been removed and in their place was various guitar cases and musical equipment, as well as other assorted luggage.

Sally took a seat by the door and Hershel sat down behind the drivers seat.

Tex stepped into the small bus and appeared even taller as he had to lower his head some to stand.

"I'm guessing you know my name. If you tell me yours I'll try to remember them."

"Oh, I'm Sally and that's Hershel."

Tex nodded to them.

"Hershel, you drive, I need some rest." Tex then walked to the back of the bus. He picked up a bottle that looked like some type whiskey and downed a large dose as Hershel moved to the drivers seat.

"Uhm, where to Tex?"

Tex sat the bottle back down.

"Head west and wake me up when we get to Weatherford." He then laid down on the makeshift bed; covering his face with his hat.

Hershel glanced at Sally. She shrugged and looked back at Tex as Hershel turned, started the bus and with a bit of gear grinding, pulled it back out onto the highway.

The old bus barely got up to forty-five miles per hour. But Sally and Hershel both felt glad to finally be moving in the direction they needed to go and have some hope of earning extra money along the way.

Soon the rain stopped and as the sun broke from the skies Tex could be heard snoring in the back.

Mile after mile the old bus chugged along until they came to a sign indicating they were entering Weatherford Oklahoma.

"You should probably wake up Tex." Hershel said.

Sally nodded and stepped back to wake the cowboy singer.

"Tex, we're coming to Weatherford."

A moan came from under the hat; then the bumpy road caused Sally to fall forward and onto the makeshift bed.

"Yeah, that's what I like, Cassy. Give me some more of that." Tex said, and then took hold of Sally in his arms and pulled her onto him.

Sally shouted, "Hey, quit that! Let go of me!" She pulled away from him and he lifted his hat up from his eyes.

"Oh, sorry Miss, but you shouldn't go sitting in my lap unless you're wanting some lovin."

"I wasn't sitting in your lap! I was trying to wake you up."

"That's a strange way to wake a feller up." He then adjusted his hat and sat up as Sally growled and moved to the front of the bus.

"What's going on back there," Hershel asked.

"He said I was sitting on his lap!" She replied.

"Well, in the mirror it did look like you was sitting on his lap. Was you or wasn't you?"

Sally growled again, "I wasn't really 'sitting' on his lap!"

Tex walked up behind her, "She was sitting on my lap. Women just have a thing for singers." He turned to Sally, "It's alright Sweet Stuff, I get it all the time."

Sally turned back to Tex with fire in her eyes.

"Pull over there at that service station." Tex said as he motioned to a station with a cafe beside it.

Once they were stopped, Tex got off first and giving the attendant some money told him, "fill'er up and check the oil." He then looked back at Hershel and continued, "you can give the change to the driver."

"Yes, sir," the attendant said and went to work.

"Maybe this'll be all right. At least Tex seems to be generous." Sally noted as she got off the bus behind Hershel.

Tex meanwhile made his way to the cafe.

After filling up the bus and adding some oil, the attendant came back out and handed Hershel twenty-three cents. Hershel and Sally looked at the change in his hand and then each other.

"I suppose it's something. We're closer to California and twenty-three cents richer than this morning." Hershel said.

Sally shook her head and made a growling sound before walking towards the cafe. Hershel put the money in his pocket and parked the bus.

In the cafe, Hershel found Tex sitting at a table, drinking coffee. He looked around but didn't see Sally. Then she walked out of the restroom and together they went to Tex's table.

Tex scooted over a little, as if to let Sally sit by him. Instead she quickly tapped Hershel's arm to get him to scoot over. She then sat next to him.

"That your girl... what did you say your name was?" Tex then took another sip of his coffee.

"Hershel, and no she's not my girl."

"Good," Tex replied and immediately turned to Sally and winked at her.

The waitress came and sat two menu's down as Sally expressed irritation due to Tex's flirting.

Sally asked for two coffee's and directly the waitress came back with them.

As Sally and Hershel looked the menu over, the waitress returned with a large steak and all the dressings; then sat it down in front of Tex.

Hershel and Sally both looked at the steak with interest. Sally then leaned forward a bit.

"So, Tex, can we order something?"

Tex began cutting the steak up.

"I'm not stopping you." He replied, while keeping his attention on the meal in front of him.

Sally's mouth twisted as this was not what she was hoping for.

After fidgeting a bit, she continued, "so, you mean the meal is on you, right?"

Tex stopped what he was doing. He looked at her and replied, "Sure, Sweet Stuff."

Sally smiled and nudged Hershel, which caused him to smile.

Tex then looked back at his meal and continued, "Just use the change from the gas."

Sally's smile immediately disappeared as the waitress walked back up.

"What'll it be?" She asked with pen and pad in hand. She then commenced to smacking her gum rather loudly.

"A hamburger with everything, and two plates," Sally replied dryly.

After he ate, Tex went to the restroom.

Sally turned to Hershel. "Why did you tell him I wasn't your girl?"

Hershel studied Sally with wonder.

"Well, you're not, are you?"

"Of course not! But now, Tex is going to be all over me!"

Hershel thought about this for a few seconds. "Well, I thought you liked him. You was the one sitting on his lap."

Daddy died when Hershel strained at this comment.

"Well, where was you planning to sit on him?"

At this point, Tex came back to the table.

"You all done? We've got a show to do."

As Hershel and Sally stepped away from the table, Tex dropped a quarter down for a tip and they walked out to the bus.

Tex drove them to a low end motel that had seen better days. He walked in as Sally and Hershel stood outside by the bus.

"Listen, we can't volunteer to spend any of our money. He offered us a job and I'm hoping that includes some of our expenses."

Hershel nodded and they watched Tex through the window as he talked to the motel clerk.

Soon he stepped outside and held up a key.

"Here you go. I'll get your costume, Sweet Stuff. You all need to get cleaned up and be ready to move out in an hour."

Sally took the key. "Just one room?"

Tex had started towards the bus but stopped.

"I'm not renting three rooms. You can stay with me if you like, Sweetheart, but otherwise you two will need to work something out."

Sally expressed a bit of shock and quickly replied, "oh, well we'll work something out, Tex. Thanks."

Tex then stepped into the bus and rummaged through the luggage. A few minutes later, he stepped back out with a rather skimpy, cowgirl outfit. On Sally's head he sat a pink cowboy hat that had a white band and white trim.

"There you are, Sweet Stuff. Wear that tonight. I'll explain what you need to do when we get there."

Sally held the outfit up and examined it with a bit of apprehension. Tex watched her briefly and then smiled and winked at her.

He then turned to Hershel. "I'll need your help with the equipment. I'll get you in on the act later."

Tex then walked to his room.

"Well, I wanted to get into show business. I guess everyone has to start somewhere." She said, still examining the small outfit with dismay.

Turning to Hershel, she straighten up the hat on her head and said, "you're sleeping on the bus! You can get cleaned up in my room, but it ain't proper for you to be in my room, unless there's no other option... you got it?"

"Yeah, I got it, Sally. And thanks for letting me get cleaned up in your room."

Sally's face twisted and she pointed her finger at him. "You better stop that right now."

"Stop what?"

"Stop trying to make me feel bad about you sleeping on the bus."

"I wasn't trying to make you feel bad. I'm happy to sleep on the bus. It's better than the ground."

"I'm warning you, Hershel, quit it right now!" Sally then turned and went into her room.

After she cleaned up and dressed, Sally came out to the bus and told Hershel he could use her room to clean up. He couldn't help but stare at her in the skimpy cowgirl outfit. She in turn gave him a questionable look and asked, "what?"

"Oh nothing, Sally... It's just that you look really nice when you're dolled up like that."

Sally's mouth opened slightly and she stared at him for several seconds. Finally she replied, "well, thank you... I think."

He then went into her room and cleaned up as well.

Later, Sally and Hershel waited on the bus. Tex eventually came out of his room. He was wearing a fresh cowboy outfit with a lot of fringe. On his head was a broad brimmed cowboy hat. He stepped onto the bus and motioned for Hershel to drive.

Tex then sat down by Sally and immediately commented on how beautiful she was. Sally's face twisted as she gave him a tight lipped smile and nod.

Hershel was given directions and told to stop at a liquor store. Once Tex had entered the store, Sally quickly moved to the seat behind Hershel. She then adjusted Hershel's footstool and several other items in a manner that would prevent her from moving over.

Tex stepped back on the bus with a large paper bag, seeming not to notice Sally had moved over. He pulled out a bottle of whiskey and took a rather large drink. He then lit up a cigarette and motioned the direction for Hershel to drive.

68

They traveled about five miles out of Weatherford.

"There's a honky-tonk up here on the right. Pull in there, that's where we'll be performing." Tex then took another drink and after putting the cap back on the bottle, he placed it in the sack and shoved in under the bench seat.

Hershel pulled into the parking lot of what he would consider a 'Bar, or Tavern.' There were many cars parked all around the outside and music could be heard from inside as Hershel shut off the engine.

"Here, take this and this." Tex handed Hershel a guitar case and a small wooden box with a lock on it. He then proceeded to sift through another stack of gear on the opposite side of the bus.

"Alright, where is it? She wouldn't have taken it... would she?" Tex seemed to be talking to himself as Hershel stood behind him.

"Oh, there you are, you beautiful little thing. We can't start the show without you!"

Tex then turned around and to Hershel's surprise, he held up a toy, stick pony. It had a cloth horse head and a stick the size of a broom handle attached to it. Tex presented it to Hershel as if it were a golden prize.

"Here take this too. And keep an eye on it, we'll be needing it soon."

Hershel took the stick pony from Tex and started off the bus. Sally waited outside the door and expressed bewilderment as Hershel walked up with the gear.

"Why are you carrying a toy horse?"

"I have no idea." He replied.

Tex then stepped out carrying a few other items.

"Alright, I'll explain the plan before we go in so you two can hear me. I play four songs during the other performer's breaks. I'll do that four or five times a night."

"Tex took hold of the stick pony and turned to Sally.

"I work for tips, so after each song I need you to ride Cinnamon here, out to the audience. Take your hat off and move around the room so they can place tips in it. If someone doesn't put a tip in, give 'em a sad face, that works at times."

He then handed the pony back to Hershel and took the small box from his hand.

"Now, after Sweet Stuff gets the tips, I need you to put them in the box and keep a close eye on it. I'll lock it and unlock it before I do my singing. You two got it?"

Sally stood looking at Cinnamon with obvious dismay. Hershel nodded as Tex handed the box back to him. Tex then took the lead into the honky-tonk.

"What's wrong?" Hershel asked Sally.

"I thought it couldn't get any worse. But it just did. He wants me to ride a toy horse."

Hershel looked at the stick pony. "Well, at least it has a nice name. I like the name Cinnamon."

They turned and walked into the loud and smoke filled honky-tonk.

"Hey, it's Tex!" The bartender shouted out, and immediately more people began to greet the singer.

After some waves and a few handshakes, Tex went to the bar and accepted a free beer.

"Are you ready to go to work? The band is just now taking a break."

Tex took a large drink from the beer and replied to the bartender, "we're ready as rain, Larry."

Larry then noticed Sally, "oh well, lookie here. You got you a new cowgirl, Tex? She's a beauty."

Tex smiled and then went over and gave Sally a one armed hug. "Ain't she precious? She likes to sit on my lap!"

Larry laughed out loud and Sally turned red. Hershel watched her mouth twist into an angry frown, but she remained quiet.

"Come on, Sweet Stuff, let's go to work!" Tex then went up to the stage, waving to people and drinking his beer along the way.

Hershel handed him the guitar. Tex then motioned for him to give Cinnamon to Sally. As soon as she took the stick horse, with

70

some reluctance, the singer stepped up to the microphone and burst into a lively song.

Sally and Hershel sat at a table off the stage and to the right of Tex. After the song, the crowd seemed to have livened up and Tex indicated Sally would be coming around for "sugar cubes, tips or any other goodies that'll fit into her hat."

Sally, rather reluctantly stood up from the table. She then mounted Cinnamon as gracefully as any woman in her twenties could mount a stick horse, and off she went.

Whoops and hollers ensued as Sally made her rounds. Tex proceeded to accompany her efforts with lively strumming on the guitar. Hershel recognized one short piece to be the overture of William Tell.

On more than one occasion Sally yelped out as one of the customers swatted her on the bottom. Eventually she made her way back to the table and poured the contents of her hat into the box. Before closing it, Hershel noted there being a lot of change, a few dollar bills, several packages of cigarettes and one large cigar.

Once again Tex belted out another lively tune and then prompted Sally to make her rounds. After four songs he stepped off the stage and a few minutes later the main singer, along with his band stepped back onto it.

As Sally poured the contents into the box, the singer on stage made some flirtatious comments concerning Sally, or, "that sweet little filly in the pink hat," as he called her.

This routine repeated four more times, until almost two o'clock in the morning. Afterwards, Sally and Hershel finally gave up on Tex, who was sitting at a table drinking with the bar owner and several other patrons.

Sally changed her clothes in the restroom and went out to the bus where Hershel had already fallen asleep on one of the bench seats.

Sometime before dawn, Tex staggered onto the bus and ordered Hershel to drive back to the motel. Once there, Tex struggled to walk, but with much teetering and several near falls, made it into his room. Sally also went to her room and Hershel went to the back of the bus and quickly fell asleep on the makeshift bed.

Whether he had an alarm clock, or just woke up naturally on time, Sally and Hershel could never be for certain. But, around fifteen minutes before checkout time, Tex came out of his room and knocked on Sally's door. She cracked it open and squinted as the sunlight streamed in and onto her face.

"Come on, Sweet Stuff. We've got to get out before noon. I'm not payin for another night." Tex held his head and winced in pain as he stated this.

"What? I've not brushed my teeth or anything!" She replied, seeming still half asleep.

"You better get your powdering done quick and get out before noon, Sugar. If'n you ain't then your payin for the extra day. And this here motel manager charges for another day at the strike of twelve."

Sally moaned in dismay and slammed the door shut. Tex staggered back to his room and soon came back out with his bags in hand. He stepped onto the bus and passed by Hershel, who was watching the events from the driver seat.

A few minutes later Sally came out of the room with everything in her arms. She got on the bus and tossed the mass of clothing and other items down on the bench seat behind Hershel.

"Hey, Sweet Stuff, be a doll and turn the keys in would you? I've got an awful headache." Tex then held his room key up.

Sally again moaned in frustration, but went back and took his key. After turning them into the front desk, she returned to the bus and immediately began organizing her belongings.

"Uhmm, where to, Tex?" Hershel asked.

"Somewhere that I can get some coffee." the singer replied with agony in his voice.

Not long after this, Hershel pulled the bus into the parking area of a small cafe. With some effort, Tex stood up and ventured in. Upon entering the establishment, he called out for some coffee and then sat at a booth table.

The waitress delivered three cups of coffee and as Tex sipped it, he appeared to feel better.

Sally and Hershel watched him and looked over the menu.

"Tex," Sally said.

"What is it, Sweet Stuff?"

"Tex, we need to get an understanding about the pay. I know you said it wouldn't be much, but we need to know what it will be so that we can budget our money accordingly."

She took another sip of her coffee and Tex rubbed his face, expressing a reluctance in talking business this early in the day.

"Well, Sugar, I'm paying for you a place to sleep. And I bought you a meal yesterday, so the expenses are fairly high already."

Sally frowned. "Tex, Hershel was given twenty-three cents yesterday from the gas. And we slept in the bus last night, for the most part. Plus you just paid for one room, Hershel is stuck sleeping on that poor excuse for a bed in the back of the bus."

Tex again rubbed his face, and then moaned with frustration.

"Are you ready to order?" The waitress asked.

"Not yet." Sally replied as Tex turned, seeming ready to get off the subject.

The waitress nodded and walked away.

"Tex, dear... we need to know how much pay we're going to get so we know how much we can spend on other necessities."

After another face rubbing episode, Tex pulled out his wallet.

"Well, I don't know how much I'll be making from one show to another. So, I can't tell you for certain. But I'll try to cut you in on the tips. I'll also pay for one meal a day. As long as it's not more than two dollars."

He then fished out six one dollar bills.

"Here, three for you and three for you."

Sally and Hershel examined the three dollars they were each given. Tex looked at Sally.

"Take it or leave it little lady. And be quick about your decision, I've got a terrible headache."

Sally glanced at Hershel. She then folded up the bills and placed them in her pocket.

"Alright Tex, we'll take the deal. At least we know where we stand now."

The three ordered their meals and ate. Tex slowly livened up but continued to drink coffee long after the meal was over. Sally got up and went to the restroom.

"That one has some fire in her. I know she's probably got her heart set on me, but I'm thinking I'm a little to old for her." Tex then sipped his coffee as he stared in the direction Sally had left in.

Hershel glanced back, as if Sally might still be visible. He then returned to his coffee.

"She sure seems to be sweet on you, Tex."

"Well, it's all part of being an entertainer. Women just can't help themselves. But, you would likely be a better choice for Sara."

Hershel broke in, "Sally."

"Yeah, Sally. I would just give her a life of heartbreak and endless road. Why don't you try to lasso her?"

Hershel considered this a few seconds.

"I don't know. I don't think she really likes me much. It seems she's mad at me most of the time. And, I really don't understand her at all."

The singer laughed, "Ain't no man can understand a woman. We were never meant to understand them. Listen, men like to take things apart, see how they work and understand what makes 'em tick. Women are what you call 'enigmas,' there ain't no figuring them out. And that's a good thing for us men. If we could figure them out, then we might lose interest."

Hershel thought about this as Tex took another drink of coffee.

"I guess I never thought of it that way."

Tex smiled, seeming to be feeling better.

"Sure, we don't need to understand 'em. We just need to appreciate 'em for what they are. The way I see it, women are... fascinating, delightful creatures, and ever single one of 'em crazy as hell."

74

Hershel smiled and then chuckled a little with Tex.

"Thanks, Tex, I appreciate the advice."

"You're welcome. I'll try to reign in my manly attraction some, so that you have a shot at her. But I can't promise anything. If'n she starts sitting in my lap again and snuggling up with me, I may not be able to restrain myself."

Hershel nodded. "Alright, but I'm not sure. I mean, we're almost like friends and I don't want to mess that up."

"Well, if that's how you feel. But don't blame me if she falls head over heels for me. I was hoping you might distract her some."

Sally came back to the table before Hershel could reply. The two men looked at her and she expressed a little unease.

"What? What are you two looking at me for? Do I have something on my face?"

Tex and Hershel chuckled again as she wiped her face with her hand.

Outside of the cafe, Tex lit a cigarette and stepped into the bus. Hershel looked down at the three dollars, which he had yet to put in his pocket.

"You were right, Sally, Tex is a generous man."

Sally turned to him. "Hershel, Tex is a skinflint. Do you know how many times I was slapped on the bottom last night and told to 'giddy up'?"

Hershel nodded, "no, how many times?"

"Well... it was a lot, I can assure you of that. And at the pay rate of three dollars, I would figure it to be around ten cents per 'giddy up.' But, as long a we're headed in the right direction and not spending our own money, then we're on the right track. I'll..., put some extra padding on before the next show. But we'll need to keep on Tex to pay us, something, anything. You got it?"

"Sure, Sally I got it. And, I would just like to say that I respect you for the fascinating, delightful and...uhm, thoughtful person that you are."

Sally stared at him for several seconds. Finally she replied.

"You should stay away from Tex's bottle. There's no helping him, but you can still make something of yourself, Hershel."

She then walked over and stepped into the bus.

The three went on to perform three to four shows per week. Sally adapted to riding Cinnamon as time went by, and as Tex shared a bit more of the tips with them, she in turn prompted more from the audience.

After they entered Texas, Hershel was given a feathered Indian headdress and a pair of buckskin pants, along with a toy tomahawk. Sally walked up to the two as Tex handed Hershel the outfit.

"Alright, I want you to put this on before the show tonight. As Sweet Stuff collects the tips, you act like your hunting for her."

Hershel examined the feathered headdress, "should I slap her on the bottom with the tomahawk? Everyone would probably like that."

Sally's face twisted.

"Now there's an idea." Tex said and seemed to be giving it some thought.

"You could sneak up behind her and slap her bottom as she's moving around the tables."

"Now, wait just.." Sally attempted to intervene.

"Or, I could tie her up and then jump up and down and holler like an Indian." Hershel said enthusiastically.

Tex nodded and became even more excited.

"She would need to be able to hold onto her hat, and at least tip toe around, you know, so they could put the tips in."

"Hey... I'm standing right here!" Sally said.

Tex put his hand up, as if to silence her.

"You could tie her up, and jump around her, hollering like an Indian brave, and then slap her bottom with the tomahawk as she struggled and moved around to take the tips. Maybe we could get you a lighter too, and you could act like you was going to set her ablaze if the audience don't give more tips. They would love that!"

76

As Hershel started to reply, Sally almost shouted. "Now wait just a minute! I think I should have some say in who ties me up and who slaps my bottom!"

Tex and Hershel turned and looked at her for a few seconds. Tex then turned back to Hershel, "We'll need some rope." Hershel smiled and nodded.

Despite Sally's reluctance, they eventually reached an agreement that allowed everything, except Hershel slapping her on the bottom.

As the new routine went into affect, the tips increased and Tex somewhat reluctantly began to share more of them with Hershel and Sally.

Unfortunately, Tex also had a habit of gambling and often lost much of his own money. On several occasions Sally and Hershel found themselves bailing him out. Tex would repay them, but it made the situation less secure for the two travelers.

Regardless of the ups and downs, the small bus pulled into Amarillo three weeks later.

"You all need to be on you're toes from here on out. The Texan's in this area can get a bit rough." Tex then stepped off the bus and went to the motel office.

"You mean to tell me it can get worse?" Sally said as she stood up and then rubbed her bottom.

"Maybe we should quit, Sally. I don't think your bottom can take much more."

Sally turned to Hershel with a very odd expression on her face.

"I'll be the one that determines how much my bottom can take... And, this whole conversation is getting a little strange."

She turned back to the front of the bus with a thoughtful expression. Hershel waited patiently. Finally she continued.

"No, let's stay with it. Tex said he could get us close to New Mexico. We've almost got enough for a bus ticket. I'll tough it out."

Hershel nodded in agreement. Then seemed to think of something.

"I've been meaning to ask you about Tex saying he wouldn't set foot in New Mexico. What did he mean by 'there's a cross bar hotel room there with his name on it'?"

Sally turned slowly back to Hershel. She stared at him for several seconds.

"You just never stop do you?"

Hershel expressed confusion.

"Stop what?"

"That!" She pointed her finger at him.

"You think I don't know what you're up to, don't you? You think that if I feel sorry for you, I'll give in, don't you? I told you Hershel, once we get to Albuquerque and get our tickets, it's good-bye. You got it? I ain't buying your act, alright? You may be a smooth talker and get your way with other girls, but I'm not an idiot!"

Hershel grimaced at the words and nodded in agreement.

"Alright Sally. I'm sorry, for, uhm, whatever I did. I'm thinking maybe I'm the idiot."

Sally appeared to come unglued.

"Listen, I've been around, alright! I know what you want me to do, you want me to say you're not an idiot, which would mean I'm the idiot!"

"No, Sally I don't want you to say I'm not an idiot. I know you've been around. I'm sure you've been around a lot more than I have."

"You better take that back right now, Mister!"

Hershel now expressed complete confusion.

"Take what back?"

"That I've been around."

"You mean you haven't been around?"

"Of course I haven't been around.. at least, not like you said it."

"How did I say it?"

Sally again pointed her finger at him.

"That's what I'm talking about. You better stop that right now." She then stormed off the bus.

Hershel sat for several minutes, trying to decipher what had happened.

Tex undoubtedly understood his audience. The crowds became rowdier at every stop once they hit Amarillo. Tex in turn seemed to lose what little self-control he had maintained to that point. Night after night, Sally and Hershel slept in the bus as Tex drank and played poker, long after the tavern or honky-tonk had closed.

It all came to a head on a Friday night, several hours after Tex had boarded the bus and woke Sally and Hershel up to "borrow" sixty dollars. Reluctantly, Sally and Hershel each loaned him thirty dollars apiece. Once Tex had exited the bus, they both leaned back into their respective seat and went back to sleep.

An hour or so later, the tavern's bartender rushed out to the bus and again woke Sally and Hershel. He spoke loudly and with urgency in his voice.

"Hey, you need to get Tex, I think he's about to get himself killed!"

The scruffy looking bartender then left the bus and went back into the large building.

Hershel tried to wake up. He glanced at Sally in the bench seat across from him and she too appeared half awake. They both stood and headed to the tavern.

Entering the dimly lit building, they were greeted by shouts. Farther inside, they found Tex and another rough looking man standing across from each other, with a table in-between. On the table sat playing cards, several bottles of whiskey and a small pile of money in the middle.

"You cheated! I know you did!" The man across from Tex yelled again.

"I did not cheat, and I'll skin you alive fer calling me a cheater!" Tex yelled back.

Both men wobbled and appeared to have drank far too much. Yet, Tex picked up a bottle and downed more as the other man sneered at him.

As Tex sat the bottle on the table with a thud, the other man yelled out, "yer dead, ya hear me? Dead!" He then turned and stormed out of the tavern.

"You all better get, if'n I know Buck, he's goin ta get his gun!'"

When the bartender said this, expressions of shock came over Hershel and Sally's face.

"Come on Tex, we need to go!" Hershel then took hold of Tex's arm.

"Now, wait just a minute," Tex said with slurred speech.

"We can't wait, Tex!" Sally almost shouted, and then turned to the bartender.

"Where's the back door?"

"It's back in the kitchen... but." Before he could finish, Sally took off towards the kitchen.

Tex took hold of the table as Hershel took him by the arm.

"I ain't goin anywhere!"

"Come on, Tex, let's go!" Hershel said and pulled him. This caused the table to fall over with a tremendous crash.

"Let go of me!" Tex shouted and fell to the ground.

Sally came back and took his other arm.

The bartender raised his hand, "Miss, you might."

Sally paid him no attention and as Tex got back to his feet she and Hershel pulled him towards the kitchen door.

They moved into the kitchen where they found a waist high counter in front of them. Pots and pans hung on hooks all around the area and straight back they could see the back door.

On closer examination, both realized the door had been boarded up. Sally let out a frustrated groan. She then turned and stepped back through the door as Hershel held Tex up, whom now seemed to be barely conscious.

"The back door is boarded up!" She shouted to the bartender.

"Yeah, well I was trying to tell you that."

At this point, she heard the front door opening and then Buck yelled out, "I'm gonna kill you... you cheater!"

Sally darted back into the kitchen before Buck rounded the corner.

"We've got to find a weapon, he's coming!" Her voice wavered with panic.

Hershel picked up a square chess grater from the counter and held it with the handle as he continued his struggle to hold Tex up.

Sally's eyes squinted as she looked at Hershel pointing the large, square grater, as if it were a pistol.

"What are you going to do with that? Grate his face off?"

Hershel shrugged his shoulders. Sally looked back and spotted a large skillet hanging from a hook.

"Where are they? Where'd they go?" Buck yelled from the other room.

She pulled it down and swung it as if getting a feel for the weight.

Hershel moved around towards the door. Sally swung it again to the other side. As she swung it, Tex was shifted around and she smacked him on the head with a loud thud. Tex slumped over unconscious and Hershel almost fell as the man's full weight pulled him down.

"Oh my God! Oh my God!!" Sally put her hand to her mouth in shock

"I hear you in there!" Buck was heard saying.

"Quick hide!" Sally said with a hushed voice.

Hershel pulled Tex around to the other side of the counter, with much effort, and then ducked behind it.

Sally raised the skillet in the air and stepped behind the door.

Buck kicked the door open and it slammed into Sally causing her to slump down in pain as the door bounced off her.

As this was happening Buck stepped into the kitchen with a small revolver in his hand.

"I know you're in here," he said, and crept up to the counter.

As he was about to look over the counter, he caught a glimpse from the corner of his eye of Sally standing back up. Hershel saw this and realized he had to do something to protect her.

Buck cocked the pistol but as he started to turn, Hershel raised up and stuck the cheese grater over Buck's hand, with the pistol in it.

The pistol and Buck's hand became lodged in the cheese grater. He couldn't fire it as the hammer was wedged as well. He growled at Hershel and reached over to pull the grater from the pistol.

At this instant, Sally raised the skillet and dropped it down on Buck's head, causing a thud and ringing sound. He fell to the ground unconscious.

"Come on Hershel, let's get out of here!" Sally dropped the skillet as Hershel nodded in agreement.

Hershel struggled to lift Tex, who became half awake and half something else.

"Let's go Tex, you've got to walk," Sally said as she tried to help Hershel.

"Wait, hold on..." Tex mumbled.

"Tex, we've got to get out of here before Buck wakes up!" Hershel then summoned an extra effort as they moved through the tavern and then out to the bus.

Upon reaching the bus, Tex again began to protest.

As they reached the door of the bus, Sally yelled out from behind, "Shut up Tex!"

Startled by her loud reprimand of Tex, Hershel turned and slammed Tex into the door, once again hitting his head and knocking him unconscious.

"Ahhh, ohhhh... I'm sorry, Tex!"

The singer was out cold again. Sally assisted in the effort to get him on board and soon they were driving away from the tavern.

Hershel got back on highway 66 and drove west until he could stay awake no longer. After finding an isolated patch of gravel beside the highway, he pulled off and went to sleep in the bench seat opposite of where Sally already lay sleeping.

"Ohh... aahhgg! Owww, what... where are we?" Tex sat up from the makeshift bed in the back of the bus. A large truck and trailer zoomed by, causing much noise and dust.

"We're a few miles west of Boise Texas." Hershel said as he sat up.

"What happened? and why does my head hurt so bad?" Tex rubbed his head again. "I've got two bumps on my noggin. What happened?"

"I'll tell you what happed, we saved your skin! And we all almost got shot doing it!" Sally replied as she tried to comb her hair with her fingers.

"Oh, I remember now. I won the pot and Buck got all upset.... Hey, where's my pot?"

Hershel and Sally looked at each other.

"What pot are you talking about, Tex?" Hershel asked, trying to sound confident.

"What pot? The pot of money on the table. You did get it, didn't you?"

Hershel again glanced at Sally. She then spoke up.

"We was a little busy saving your life, Tex. Buck came after you with a gun!"

Tex stood up and stormed to the front of the bus.

"You left my money? That was my money you left on the table!"

"Your money? Don't forget you borrowed thirty dollars from me and Hershel both!" Sally said.

"Yeah, well you left it too, on the table with my hundred dollars!"

"We was busy saving your life, Tex!" She replied.

"I was doin fine until you two barged in!" Tex then put his hand on his head again, seeming to be in pain.

"I can't believe it! That's the thanks we get for saving his life!" She said, looking at Hershel.

Hershel nodded a bit, but otherwise tried to stay out of it.

"What hit my head?" Tex leaned over to the rear view mirror and examined the two bumps.

"You uhm, sort of ran into a door... and a skillet." Hershel replied meekly.

"Ahhggg, I can't believe this." Tex paused in thought and then continued, "well, you two are goinna have to go back to Boise with me. You owe me a hundred dollars."

Sally almost shouted, "we owe you? First, you borrowed sixty dollars from me and Hershel, so you owe us thirty dollars apiece! Second, we saved your pathetic life! Buck would have shot you if we hadn't got you out of there!"

Tex now spoke loudly as well.

"Listen Sweet Stuff, there was almost two hundred dollars on that table, and it was mine, fair and square! So you and Hershel's sixty dollars was on that table with my hundred plus dollars! And the way I see it, you two should have stayed on the bus! I've been in worse situations than that!"

The two sneered at each other for several seconds.

"We ain't going back to Boise with you, Tex. Maybe you get a gun pulled on you and get shot at on a regular basis, but Hershel and I don't get ourselves shot at. Ain't that right Hershel?"

Hershel squinted and then replied with a meek voice.

"Uhm, well other than that one time outside of Oklahoma City, no we don't normally get shot at."

Sally glanced at Hershel, then back to Tex. "Other than that one time outside of Oklahoma City, we don't get shot at!"

For several more seconds they stared at each other. Then Tex spoke.

"If that's the way you feel about it, then you two can just get on your way to California. I've got to go make some money and I ain't making any here on the side of the highway."

Hershel watched the two of them as they stood glaring at each other again. Then Sally growled and turned to Hershel.

"Come on Hershel, that's the thanks we get for saving his life... getting kicked off the bus."

The two rounded up their belongings and stepped off and onto the side of the highway. As Tex sat down in the driver's seat, Hershel waved bye to him.

Tex grimaced a little and then said, "Sorry partner, but we would have split the crew up sooner or later anyway. There's no way I'm setting foot in New Mexico."

Hershel nodded as Sally worked beside him to get her baggage together. Tex then shut the door of the bus. He turned it around and headed east.

As dust and exhaust fumes floated around the two, Sally picked up her makeshift baggage and started walking west. Hershel slung the footstool over his shoulder; picked up his other things and moved quickly to catch up with her.

"I can't believe it! He just drops us off in the middle of nowhere!" Sally grumbled as she trudged along.

"Uhm, well we are a lot closer to California though." He replied, while readjusted his luggage and struggling to catch up.

"He took us for sixty bucks, Hershel! Now we're almost back to square one!"

Sally then stuck her thumb out as a car came close and zoomed by.

"He did try to tell us about the money on the table."

Sally stopped and turned around.

"Are you taking up for him?"

Hershel stopped and lifted the strap on the foot stool for some relief from the weight.

"I'm just trying to be fair. Tex helped us get a lot farther than where we were when we met him. And even though we lost sixty dollars, we have a little more than we did when we was sitting at the gas station where he hired us."

Sally stared at Hershel. She stuck her thumb out again as another car went by. Dust flew around them and she put her hand back down.

Hershel waited patiently. Finally Sally spoke with a sarcastic tone.

"His real name is Chester."

Hershel squinted as he considered this.

"How do you know that?"

"I saw it on some paperwork in the bus." She replied.

"Well, so what? What does that have to do with anything?"

Sally started walking again, but said, "you going to trust a guy that's named Chester?"

Hershel came up beside her.

"Why wouldn't I? What do you have against Tex... or Chester? I thought you liked him, you was sitting on his lap... or wherever it was that you was sitting on him."

Sally grimaced.

"I don't trust him because he's a man. I know what men want. The first mistake a woman makes is to trust a man. You may think 'old Chester' is good as gold but I ain't falling for that. He took us for sixty dollars and left us in the middle of nowhere. He may have been your buddy, but I'm not that easy!"

Hershel followed her for several miles. Finally, they got a ride with what looked to be a farmer, in a pick-up. Still, neither one spoke as they crossed into New Mexico.

Chapter Six: The Generous Wisdom of Libby

Several rides into New Mexico, a farmer dropped them off and they once again walked along the dusty highway.

After an hour or so, a large green sedan slowed and stopped. The two moved quickly to the car.

"You two need a ride?"

"Most defiantly," Sally replied to the man.

"Well, just put everything in the back there," He said to Hershel and then stuck a cigar back into his mouth.

As Hershel put their belongings in the back seat, the man insisted on Sally sitting in front with him, forcing Hershel to sit in the back with their luggage.

The car moved back onto the rode and the man immediately struck up a discussion with Sally. He introduced himself as Edgar, a salesman.

Hershel sat in the back listening as Edgar and Sally talked and laughed. She seemed to be in her element as she fended off his advances one after the other, with a delicate grace that neither forced him to stop nor encouraged him to continue.

Finally, as the sun settled on the horizon, the large sedan rolled into San Jon, New Mexico.

"You need to get a room, Sally?" Edgar had it seemed totally forgotten about Hershel in the back seat.

Sally smiled, "Are you staying in San Jon, Edgar? Which motel are you staying at?" She replied with a sweet tone.

"Well, there's only two in town. The San Jon or Roadrunner motel, but they're both nice motels. Which one do you want to stay at?"

Hershel cringed as Edgar seemed to have Sally cornered.

"Oh, Edgar, we don't need a room, we have friends to stay with. I just wanted to know which one you was staying at, in case we wanted to visit." Again she smiled.

Edgar glanced back at Hershel, seeming to sorely recall there being two hitchhikers.

"Well, if you want to visit, Sally, I'll be at the San Jon. I can drop you off at your friends house if you want."

"No, that's alright. Just drop us off at the cafe there. I want to freshen up a little and give them a call first, you know, give them time to tidy up."

"Well, alright then. The San Jon motel is about a quarter mile on up, if you want to visit," Edgar said, as he pulled up to the cafe.

"Oh, alright, I'll remember that." Sally said.

The sedan stopped and Hershel shook his head in disbelief. Sally got out and Hershel gathered up their luggage and got out as well.

"Bye Sally, remember, the San Jon. Just ask for my room at the front counter. They'll give you the room number."

"Oh don't worry, Edgar dear, I won't forget." Sally replied and waved a little wave.

As the large sedan moved away, Hershel asked, "we don't have any friends in San Jon, do we?"

"Of course not. I just wanted to make sure there was more than one motel in town. We'll ask where the Roadrunner is inside." She then went into the cafe. They split a hamburger and then proceeded to the Roadrunner motel.

The following morning, they went back to the cafe. They ate some toast and drank coffee, but also kept an eye out for Edgar.

As they began to walk through town after breakfast, Hershel stopped by a small hardware store and bought a flashlight and batteries. Then they continued cautiously past the San Jon to make sure Edgar's sedan was gone. After assuring themselves that he'd already left, they moved on out of town.

The rest of the day consisted of walking and catching a few rides from local farmers or residents, which amounted to anywhere from three to ten miles each. As the sun settled on the horizon, Sally and Hershel were dropped off at a motel in Tucumcari.

"These motels are eating up our money." Sally then grunted with distaste as they moved towards the office.

"You want to find the bus stop and sleep there?" Hershel replied as he got a better hold on his grandmother's urn and then adjusted the footstool.

Sally glanced at him, as if considering it.

"No, it's a ways between here and Santa Rosa. We need to wash some clothes and I want a bath before we get on that long stretch."

Later, after getting checked into their rooms, Hershel walked down to a cafe and ordered a meal to go as Sally began washing clothes.

The following day they waited until a few minutes before check out time to leave as some of their clothes had still not dried. As they made their way out of Tucumcari, Hershel held a pair of pants and one of Sally's blouses in the air in a attempt to finish drying them with the warm breeze.

For an hour they walked along the highway and had no luck catching a ride. As it grew close to noon and the sun beat down on them, a large Buick, that Hershel thought to be an early nineteen fifties model, pulled to the side of the road.

"You two kids needing a ride?" An elderly woman asked. She had her hair in a bun and wore white, horn rimmed glasses. The small woman seemed to be almost swallowed up by the steering wheel and dash of the large Buick.

"Yes Ma'am we surely do." Hershel replied into the half open passenger side window.

"You young-uns get in, I can take you around thirty miles farther down the road."

The two put their belongings in the back seat. Sally climbed in the front and as Hershel began to get into the back, the woman glanced back and said, "you can sit up here with us young man. There's plenty of room here for the both of you."

Hershel nodded and after shutting the back door sat down next to Sally. Once the door was closed, the woman moved the old Buick back onto the highway and slowly got up to around fifty miles per hour.

"So where are you young folks headed to?"

"Hollywood," Sally replied.

Hershel leaned over slightly, "Los Angeles."

"Oh," the woman said, never turning from the road.

"My name is Libby. I live about, thirty miles from here. I'll take you that far and maybe you can get a ride from there."

"That would be wonderful. I'm Sally and this is Hershel. We're very happy to meet you, and thanks for the lift."

After a slow, but steady ride, the woman pulled into the drive of a large house, which sat around twenty yards from the highway.

"This is my house. I live here alone now. My dear husband, Royce, passed away ten years ago. So it's just me now and this big old house. But, I like the peace and quiet."

The three got out of the car and soon Hershel had their baggage together.

"Thank you again, Libby," Sally said as the two started to walk towards the highway.

"You're welcome dear. I wish you and Hershel luck." She then opened up the trunk of the Buick and Hershel noticed it was loaded with groceries.

He stopped and nodded to the car. Sally turned and looked at Libby as she struggled to get a large brown paper sack out of the trunk.

"Here Libby, let me help you." Hershel sat his stuff down and went over to help with the groceries.

Sally shook her head, let out a disgruntled sigh and then went over to help as well.

"Oh, thank you Hershel. I always have trouble with this part of it. Once they're inside, I can put the things up."

When all the groceries were in, the two started towards the door.

"Bye Libby. And thanks again for the ride." Sally said with a little wave.

"You're very welcome, Sally." She paused and seemed to think of something. "Have you two eaten lately? I was about to cook some dinner. You should eat something before you go."

"Well, uhm." Sally hesitated.

"That would be wonderful, Libby. If you're sure it's not too much trouble." Hershel said and glanced at Sally, who squinted her eyes in frustration. Hershel smiled at her and walked towards the kitchen.

"Can I help you, Libby?"

"Do you like to cook, Hershel?"

"I do, I used to cook for my grandmother all the time."

"Well, that would be very nice. My Royce, he loved to cook as well."

Sally walked back into the living room as Hershel and Libby went into the kitchen. She sat her stuff down and then sat on the couch. Within a few seconds of sitting down, several large cats were in her lap. She pushed them onto the floor but they immediately jumped back into her lap. After five or six times of being shoved off her lap, the cats gave up and wandered off..

In the kitchen, Hershel washed his hands and began assisting Libby. As he was pealing potatoes, Libby asked him, "so, is Sally your girlfriend?"

`Hershel winced at the thought and almost cut himself.

"Oh, no, not at all. In fact I think she can barely put up with me."

Libby smelled the contents of a sauce pan she was tending.

"Why would you say that? You seem like a fine young man. And Sally seems like a very nice young woman. She's very pretty and polite."

Hershel focused on his potato peeling, but uttered under his breath, "let's not forget crazy..."

"What was that?" Libby asked

"Oh, uhm, and caring, she, really cares about herself and others...occasionally."

"I see, well then you two should get along well. What prompted the two of you to travel together? If you don't mind me asking."

Hershel moved over to the sink and began washing the potatoes he had peeled.

"We just, sort of met on the side of the road in Oklahoma. She'd just been dropped off by a "pig" and my car along with most of my money had recently been stolen. So, I suppose it was convenient for us to travel together."

"Hhmm, that's interesting." Libby stirred the contents of the saucepan but also studied Hershel carefully.

"You know, Hershel, women are not always easy to understand. Sometimes, we put a wall up and do things that can, well, seem odd. It's a type of defense mechanism I think. I'm sure I often frustrated my husband Royce, to no end. Perhaps, if Sally should ever frustrate you, you could consider that."

Hershel, turned back to Libby. He thought about what she said as he washed the last potato and placed it in a bowl.

"I will, Libby. And thanks for the advice."

Libby smiled and nodded to Hershel.

After dinner, Hershel and Sally once again gathered their things together. Libby followed behind them to the door.

"Thanks again Libby. That was a wonderful dinner." Sally then opened the door to a warm evening sky.

"Oh my, it's almost dark. You two shouldn't be traveling at night. Why don't you stay here tonight. You can leave bright and early in the morning."

Hershel and Sally looked outside and then back to each other.

"That's very kind of you, but we don't want to be any more trouble." Sally replied.

"It's no trouble, dear. I have a spare room and as long as Hershel doesn't mind sleeping on the couch, we'll manage just fine."

Again, Sally glanced at Hershel.

"I don't mind at all. And it would be nice if we could clean up." He said.

"Oh yes, certainly you can both clean up. I'll get some blankets and a pillow together for you, Hershel."

Sally smiled slightly and then shut the door.

"Let me help you, Libby," Sally said and followed her to the back room.

The following morning Sally woke up, stretched; got dressed and stepped out of the spare room. After a stop at the bathroom, she began following the smell of fresh brewed coffee.

Easing through the living room, she chuckled at the sight of Hershel asleep on the couch with a large furry cat laying on his chest.

Entering the kitchen she found Libby in a housecoat and pouring a cup of coffee.

"Good morning, dear. Hopefully I didn't wake you."

"No, I slept great. I don't think I've slept that well in weeks."

Libby smiled. "Would you like a cup of coffee?"

"That would be fantastic." She then sat down at the table as Libby got another cup for Sally.

Once they were both sat down, Libby sipped her coffee and glanced over to Sally.

"Hershel tells me you two have been traveling together all the way from Oklahoma."

Sally grunted under her breath. "Yeah, it's been quite the trip so far. Not the one I had planned, that's for sure."

"Really, so what did you have planned?"

Sally glanced at Libby, seeming reluctant to talk about it. After another sip of coffee, she replied in a soft voice.

"Well, this guy from my home town was suppose to take me to Albuquerque. From there I was going to get a bus out to Hollywood and still have enough money to get by for a while." She then paused.

"You mean the "pig?" Libby asked.

Sally grimaced with the thought.

"Yeah, he was that alright. We got a few hundred miles from home and the deal suddenly changed. What a Jackass, I hope he had five blowouts on his way to Albuquerque."

Libby smiled and took another sip of her coffee.

"It's a good thing you met Hershel. He seems to be a nice young man."

Sally glanced at Libby again.

"Yeah, but he's a man. And men want one thing. I know what they want, and they'll do anything to get it. Including playing 'Mr. Nice Guy.' I don't trust any of them." She paused and her head lowered a bit. "I went through a bad case of love three years ago. It led to noting but heartache."

Libby smiled again as she held her coffee with both hands. After a few seconds of silence she replied.

"You know, if men didn't want that one thing from us women, we might have trouble getting their attention. They would tinker with their machines and such. Or go hunting and fishing all the time. We might miss it if they didn't find at least one thing about us irresistible." She paused and then continued. "And, I'm a firm believer in the old saying, 'don't throw the baby out with the bath water.' One bad experience with love doesn't mean the next one will be the same."

Sally appeared to be in thought. She took another drink of her coffee.

"Maybe your right, but I don't have time for that kind of stuff anyway. I'm going to Hollywood to be an actress. Nice men want women to marry and set up a home with five kids. That's not what I want and I'm not letting a man lock me into it, even if he is a, 'decent guy'."

Again silence held the small kitchen. Finally Libby replied.

"It's been my experience, that there are some men, a few anyway, that have a heart large enough to care about the woman's dreams as well as his own. These men will do what they can to help the woman they love in achieving their dreams. But there's not many of these men around, and if you should come across one, you might not want to let him get away."

Sally stared at Libby for several, silent seconds.

94

"I don't know, Libby. I can't think about all of that now. And besides, as soon as we get to Arizona, we're parting ways."

Libby expressed disappointment.

"That's too bad. You've done fairly well so far, it seems."

"Yeah, well, I'm catching a bus in Winslow and that's the end of our 'mutual agreement'."

Libby took another drink of her coffee, then replied.

"I've always wanted take a bus trip. But I'm sure they wouldn't let my cats come with me..." She stopped and stared into space.

"What?" Sally asked.

Libby almost shook as she pulled back from her thoughts. "Oh, nothing dear. Uhm, I need to get a few things together. You help yourself to the coffee. There should be enough for Hershel as well; when he wakes up."

Libby then left the kitchen.

Hershel woke shortly after this with the swishing of a cat's tail in his face. After several stifled sneezes and a visit to the bathroom he was also sitting at the kitchen table, drinking coffee.

"So, Libby didn't say where she was going?" He asked and then took another drink of his coffee.

"No, she just said she had some things to get together. And, we should help ourselves to the coffee."

A few minutes later, Libby stuck her head into the door of the kitchen.

"Oh, Hershel, you're awake. Would you be a dear and prepare some breakfast for us? I'm just, uh, tending some things. I'll be in shortly." She then darted back out.

Hershel glanced at Sally, who shrugged her shoulders. Hershel stood up and then went to work preparing breakfast for the three.

As he finished placing the last of the fried eggs on a plate, Libby came in. She smiled and appeared slightly winded.

"Oh, that smells so good, Hershel. You are a great cook, don't you think so, Sally?" She then tucked a lose strand of hair behind her ear and sat at the table.

As they ate, Libby did most of the talking.

"You know, adversity can bring out the best in people. Royce and I went through some very tough times together, but it also sharpened us up and forced us to work as a team."

Hershel smiled and took another bite. He glanced over to Sally and she had an odd expression on her face, as if Libby might be a little off, mentally.

"Children can really rouse the best in us as well. Having responsibility for little ones that depend on us for everything, can build character and strengthen bonds between two people." She paused and after looking at both Sally and Hershel, continued. "Don't you agree?"

"Uh, yeah, sure, Libby. That's right, wouldn't you say so, Hershel?"

Hershel was drinking the last of his milk, but quickly lowered the glass and wiped his mouth with a napkin.

"Absolutely, those are true words of wisdom, Libby."

"Good, I'm glad you both agree. I feel you are both wonderful young people and....well, if the two of you were to really work together, you would see just how important your friendship is."

Hershel noticed that Sally's face had once again twisted into the odd expression of questioning Libby's sanity.

"That's very... poetic, Libby. You really remind me of my grandmother, right before she... well, anyway... speaking of children; do you have any that come and check on you from time to time?" Sally then gently put her hand on Libby's arm.

The elderly woman smiled with this show of concern. "Oh, yes dear I have children that check on me, as well as neighbors that stop by. You're very sweet to think of such a thing."

Silence held the room for a few seconds and then Sally stood up.

"I suppose we need to go, Hershel." She then turned to Libby, "thank you for everything. We really appreciate it."

"Well, you're very welcome Sally and I've gathered a few things together that you two might find useful," she glanced back at them as she stood up and continued; "or helpful anyway. I just feel the two of you need some...things."

96

"Libby, you don't need to do anything else, you've already helped enough." Hershel said as the elderly woman started towards the back door.

"Nonsense, you two go ahead to the living room and I'll meet you in there." With that Libby went to the back of the house while Hershel and Sally moved to the living room.

Soon Libby came through the door with a wicker styled case that had a handle for carrying. She sat it on the coffee table and opened it as Hershel and Sally stood by the front door.

"I thought you two could use a few more clothes. Hershel looks to be the same size as my dear Royce, and I was once your size... and shape, Sally."

She then pulled out a pair of pants that was obviously a number of decades out of style. They appeared to be part of the famed Zuit suit era as the waist came up very high.

Sally couldn't help but giggle under her breath. Libby folded the pants and continued.

"There's another pair in here Hershel and a couple of nice shirts. I also put a few dresses in here for you Sally."

Libby pulled out an equally out of date dress and held it up for Sally to see.

"Oh, my goodness, I danced so many times in this one. You two should have seen Royce and me on the dance floor back then."

Sally's face dropped a bit as she appeared to imagine herself in the dress. Then she buffered up and asked, "What dance was that Libby, the Charleston?"

"Yes! How did you ever know?"

Sally glanced at Hershel, who smiled slightly.

"It was just a good guess." Sally replied.

Libby smiled and then went on.

"There's also two bottles filled with water in here, just in case you get thirsty." She paused and glanced back at the two. Then continued. "Well, I hope you find everything in here helpful. And remember what I said about working together."

"We will Libby and thank you for the clothes." Hershel walked over and took the wicker case.

A few more good-byes ensued and then the two went to the highway and after a short wait got a ride in the back of a pickup truck. The air was dry and warm but the two leaned back and enjoyed the beautiful sunrise.

Chapter Seven: Put that thing Away!

The day progressed and they only managed to get a few short rides. They eventually found themselves in the middle of nowhere and the sun quickly descending towards the horizon.

"There's a building up there. We better hurry or we'll be on the side of the road in the dark." With that comment, Sally began to walk quicker and Hershel followed behind, struggling with his makeshift luggage.

As they neared the structure in the twilight of the evening, the two could see it was a barn off to the side of the highway. Once they were beside it they looked at each other with dismay.

"It's going to have to do. It's a good thing you bought that flashlight." Sally started towards the barbed wire fence.

"We can't stay there!"

Sally stopped before attempting to get through the fence.

"Why not?"

"We'll be trespassing." He replied in a nervous voice.

Sally's mouth twisted in frustration.

"Fine, you give me the flashlight. I'll sleep in the barn and you sleep out here on the side of the road."

Hershel considered this as he examined Sally's outstretched hand. Finally he walked to the fence and pulled two strands of barbed wire apart for Sally to get through.

"I don't like it. I feel like a criminal."

Once Sally was on the other side, she chuckled and watched him struggle through with his unwieldy burdens.

"Hershel, you ever heard the saying 'desperate times call for desperate measures'?"

After getting caught on the barbed wire several times and then unhooking himself, Hershel stood up and answered.

"Yeah, I've heard of that. But I didn't think it included trespassing."

Sally laughed a bit, picked up her stuff and walked to the barn.

Stepping inside, they found the building full of square hay bales, along with a large pile of hay in the middle.

"Well, it's indoors and dry at least. Give me the flashlight."

Hershel fished out the flashlight and handed it to her. They crept over to the hay stack just as the last bit of daylight gave way to night.

Sally shined the light all around the area that she planned to sit down at before actually sitting. Finally, after confirming there were no snakes or spiders about, she plopped down in the hay and leaned back, as if exhausted.

Hershel sat down not far from her and pulled something to eat from a shirt that Sally had tied up to make a bag.

"Do we still have some crackers?" Sally asked, seeming very tired.

"Yeah, I'll get some for you." Hershel started to reach into the shirt again when a scratching sound was heard.

"What is that?" Sally sat up.

"I don't know."

They both sat very still. Soon another scratching sound came from very close. Then a muffled "eeeowww" was heard.

Sally moved closer to Hershel and began shining the flashlight around.

"Where's it coming from?" She asked.

"I don't know...shhh."

Again they both sat still. After a few seconds the scratching sound was heard again and then another muffled, "eeooww."

Sally shined the light on the wicker case that Libby had given them.

"It's coming from there," she said and held the light on it.

Hershel crept over to the case. He unlatched and opened the top. Then he carefully pulled the clothing out one piece at a time. Sally moved closer and held the light up.

At the bottom of the case Hershel found a wooden box with holes on the sides. He lifted it out of the case and as he did so they heard another, "eeowww," from inside the box.

The two looked at each other and Hershel then slid the lid on the box open to reveal a fluffy gray kitten inside.

"Eeeoowww," it then looked up at Hershel and Sally, whom again glanced at each other.

"Great, another mouth to feed." Sally then moved back to her original location.

Hershel took the kitten out of the box and began petting it. He then looked back in the wicker case and pulled out a brown paper bag.

After opening it up, he said "Libby sent some food for it."

Sally huffed under her breath. "Yeah, and how long is that going to last? What was she thinking, giving us a cat?"

"It's really cute. You wanna hold it?"

Sally smirked and replied, "Nooo.... I don't wanna hold it!" She lay back down. "Your taking care of that thing, not me. And where's my crackers?"

Hershel began searching for the crackers but whispered to the kitten, "don't worry, her bark is worse than her bite."

"I heard that..." Sally said.

The following morning Sally woke up to find the kitten laying on her chest.

"Ahhggg, Hershel, get your cat off of me." She sat up a little and the kitten slid down to her cleavage.

Hershel woke up and moved over to get the kitten. As his hand got closer to her chest, he seemed to wake up enough to noticed where his hand was going. He stopped a few inches away from the kitten.

"Uhmm, are you sure you want me to get it?"

Sally gave him a sleepy look of frustration and snapped, "yes, I want you to get it, what did I just say?"

Hershel began to slowly move his hand closer; Sally suddenly seemed to realize just where the kitten was perched.

"Wait! No, I'll uhm, I'll get it. Never mind."

Hershel pulled his hand back, appearing relieved. Sally reached up and took the kitten in her hand. She raised it up as it began to purr. After a brief examination, she handed it to Hershel.

"It's cute, right?" He asked.

Sally huffed and stood up. She then began to brush the hay off of her.

Soon they were back on the highway trying to catch a ride. Within a half hour, a farmer driving a tractor stopped. He was pulling a trailer with several bails of hay on it.

"I can get you a few miles down the road, if you don't mind riding on the trailer," he said.

"That would be great," Sally replied and they climbed onto the trailer.

After a few minutes, Hershel got the kitten out and was hand feeding it.

Sally watched with a frown.

"We're not keeping that... thing. It's got to go, you know that don't you?"

Hershel looked at Sally as a breeze blew small bits of hay around.

"Why? It's just a kitten. I'll take care of it."

Sally grunted and turned her head.

Later, they caught a ride with a truck driver. The three sat in the front of the truck as it rolled noisily down the road.

Hershel opened the wicker case and pulled the kitten out. Sally huffed about this.

"Isn't this the cutest little kitten?" Hershel held it up, right in front of Sally's face to show the truck driver.

"Well, ain't that the sweetest little thing." The rough looking truck driver said.

Sally moved her head back.

The truck driver stuck the cigar he was holding in his right hand into his mouth and then took the little kitten.

"Ohhh, my daughter would just love this."

"You can have it!" Sally said.

"Oh, well, I would love to give it to her and thank you all the same, but we live in apartments with no pets allowed."

Hershel looked at Sally and squinted his eyes. Sally squinted her eyes as well, in an exaggerated manner; as the truck driver handed the kitten back to Hershel.

Later, the two stood alongside the highway not far from an isolated gas station, which they had been let out at from a previous ride.

It was afternoon by now and the day was hot and dry.

An elderly woman noticed the two as an attendant serviced her large sedan.

After paying for her gas, the woman pulled the car up to Sally and Hershel. The windows were rolled up, so Sally walked around to the driver's side and the woman rolled the window down.

"Do you two need a ride?"

"Yes, please, if you don't mind." Sally replied.

"Oh I don't mind. I hate to see people standing out in this heat. You'll need to ride in the back though; I have my hat box up here with me. There should be plenty of room in the back for both of you."

"Thank you," Sally replied and soon the two were loaded into the back seat with their odd assortment of luggage.

Hershel sat the wicker case on the floor board between his feet. After shutting his door, the woman slowly pulled the large vehicle back onto the highway.

"So where are you two headed?" She asked and glanced into the rear view mirror.

The woman examined the two and could see the faces and upper chest area of both Sally and Hershel.

Sally smiled and replied, "California."

"Oh that's nice," The woman then looked back at the road.

"It's really nice that you have air-conditioning. It feels great." Sally said.

The elderly woman again glanced into her rear view mirror.

"Yes, it is very nice. I bought this car last year. I decided to splurge a little and go with the air-conditioning. I'm glad that I did." She then looked back to the road.

A few minutes later, Hershel reached into the wicker case and pulled the kitten out. Sally glanced at him and frowned.

Soon, he was playing with the kitten in his lap. A smile broke over his face as he tickled the cat's tummy and it would bat at his fingers with it's tiny paws.

"Would you put that thing away? Every time I turn around you've got it out... playing with it." Sally said.

The woman glanced up into her mirror and could clearly see Hershel smiling and doing something in his lap. Sally, however was looking down in Hershel's lap with a slight expression of disgust.

"It needs attention, Sally. You won't even touch it. It's not natural to leave it closed up in the dark all the time."

The woman now had trouble keeping her eyes on the road. She kept her head facing forward but her eyes inevitably moved to the mirror.

"Yeah, I know what you want. You want me touch it and hold it, don't you? I know why you keep getting it out, you want me to look at it; get all emotional and then start holding it, don't you?"

Sally again glanced back into Hershel's lap as he continued to smile and do something.

"What's wrong with that, Sally? Like I said, it needs attention; if you're not going to give it any, then I will. You see how it perks up when I get it out. It needs love and affection."

The elderly woman swallowed hard and her grip tightened on the steering wheel. Hershel continued.

"Come on, Sally, you don't have to play with it, but at least hold it."

"I've told you, Hershel, I don't want to touch it, or hold it. And I'm certainly not going to play with it. I wish you would just put it back where it belongs."

The woman readjusted herself in the seat. She nervously moved a stray hair from her face and struggled to keep her eyes on the road. As she glanced back in the mirror, Sally had turned away from Hershel, who was still smiling and doing something in his lap.

"I know why you don't want to hold it."

Sally turned to Hershel and again, glancing in his lap asked, "why?"

"Because you know you'll like it. And if you like it, then you'll start playing with it, and then you'll like that as well."

Sally glanced up at Hershel and then back down to his lap as he continued his mysterious activity; smiling even wider.

A few seconds went by and the car swerved slightly as the woman realized she was almost off the road.

She glanced back in the mirror and noticed the two look up briefly, but then return to their discussion.

"Yeah, fine... you got me. That's why I don't want to hold it." Sally then turned away from Hershel's lap and faced the window.

"Was that so hard to admit, Sally. Don't you feel better now? You really should hold it, just for a few minutes. It won't bite you. It just wants a little love."

The woman could barely focus on her driving now as she saw Sally look back into Hershel's lap.

Slowly a slight smile broke over her face. "Well... it is kinda cute, isn't it?" Sally said.

Suddenly the car pulled to the side of the road.

"Uhmm, you two need to get out now. This is as far as I can take you."

Hershel put the kitten back into the case as Sally looked around.

"Right here? Are you going any further?" Sally asked.

The woman didn't turn around but replied nervously, "no, I'm turning right up here a ways, you two please get out now."

"Well, alright, thank you for the ride." Sally then nudged Hershel. He opened the door and they climbed out with their luggage.

As soon as Hershel shut the door, the car drove away quickly, causing the tires to squeal on the pavement.

The two looked around and found there wasn't a building or house in sight.

"That was sure strange. She just dropped us off in the middle of nowhere." Sally said

"Yeah, real strange." Hershel replied.

They gathered their things up and began walking west, eventually catching another ride.

Chapter Eight: Buttercups on a Marmalade Sea

Long after the sun had set, the two were dropped off at an intersection in Santa Rosa.

Spotting a truck stop several blocks away, they wearily made their way down the street.

Once inside, a waitress in her mid-thirties brought them a couple glasses of water and two menus.

"Thank you," Hershel said as the waitress walked away.

"We've got to watch our money. At this rate, we'll be broke before we get to Arizona." Sally then took a drink of her water and began to examine the menu.

"We can ask the waitress where the bus station is." Hershel replied, then took a drink of water as well.

A man walked over to the jukebox and dropped a dime in. As Sally considered Hershel's idea, a country and western song began to play.

"Yeah... let's split a hamburger with fries. We can ask where the bus stop and maybe the park is. Between the two, one should be close enough to walk to."

A few seconds after Sally said this, the waitress came and took their order. She then gave them directions to the bus station as well as the city park. Both were walking distance from the cafe.

Hershel wrapped up a few of his French fries in a napkin and placed them in his pocket before they left the cafe.

After walking six blocks through the city, they arrived at the bus station. Both sat down on the bench outside the station.

Sally appeared to be exhausted, she slumped at the end of the bench with her head leaning against the wall.

Hershel watched her briefly and then opened the wicker case to get the kitten out.

He held the little cat and fed it a French fry. As he was about to feed it another one, he glanced over and noticed Sally watching him.

Without saying anything, he offered the kitten and French fry to her. She stared at it for several seconds. Then she shook her head, but also reached out and took them.

As a noisy bus rolled into the station, Sally fed the kitten, and soon Hershel noticed a slight smile break across her face.

Later, Sally went into the building. After walking around a bit, she located the restroom and went in to clean up some. She came back out fifteen minutes later and headed outside to get Hershel. The man behind the ticket counter watched her closely.

"Alright Hershel, it's your turn. The restrooms are over towards the right, in the corner."

Hershel nodded, then placed his stuff on the bench and went in to clean up.

As he left the bus station later, the man at the counter watched him closely as well.

Soon Sally and Hershel were asleep on the bench.

Sometime after midnight, they were roused awake by the tap of a night stick.

"Are you two waiting for a bus?"

Hershel opened his eyes to see a policeman staring down at them.

Sally was also sitting up; rubbing her eyes.

"Uhm, no officer, we're uh, just resting for a bit, Sir."

The officer stared at Hershel after he said this. He then glanced over at Sally.

"Well, you can't rest here unless you're waiting for a bus. There's no loitering."

"Oh, alright, we didn't know."

Hershel stood up.

"Come on, Sally, we can't stay here." Hershel then began to pick their belongings up.

As they walked away from the bus station, Sally moaned with frustration.

"Where are we going?" She asked as she followed behind Hershel.

He glanced back and noticed the patrolman getting into his squad car.

"I'm not sure yet."

"What do you mean you're not sure? I'm tired, Hershel." Sally struggled to keep up.

"Just hang on."

As they got several blocks away from the bus station, Hershel glanced back and noticed the policeman was following them in his car.

"Ahhgg, he's following us. That's what I was afraid of." After he said this, Sally glanced back.

"Don't look at him, he'll get even more suspicious."

Sally huffed, "I'm sorry, I'm tired. It's the middle of the night. Maybe he'll take us to jail and we can get some sleep."

"Hold on, I've got a plan." Hershel then started to walk faster.

"Slow down!" Sally shifted her blouse bag from one arm to the other and moved faster to keep up.

A few minutes later they arrived in front of a motel.

"We can't get a room, Hershel, we've got to save some money." Sally whined.

Hershel looked back to the policeman, who was creeping towards them in the patrol car.

"I know, just follow my lead. Wait until he gets closer."

Slowly the patrol car moved closer to them. Once Hershel felt it was close enough, he stepped into the motel office.

A bell attached to the top of the door rang. Hershel glanced out the window and saw the patrol car was setting a short distance away.

Soon a man came from the back room. He had obviously just got out of bed as he wore a robe and looked as if he'd simply ran his fingers through his hair.

"Can I help you?"

Hershel glanced out the window again, the patrol car was still there.

"How much is a room?"

"Six dollars." The man said and then rubbed his head.

Hershel noticed the patrol car slowly moving from its parked position.

"Do you have anything cheaper?" Hershel asked and nodded towards the window to Sally. She glanced out the window just as the police car was turning the corner and driving away. She looked back at Hershel and smiled.

"You're not going to find anything cheaper, anywhere." The man replied.

"Oh, well, I'm real sorry we bothered you."

The man grunted and gave Hershel an aggravated stare. He then turned and went into the back room as Hershel and Sally left the office.

"Very clever. But what's the plan now?"

Hershel scanned the street to be sure the policeman was gone.

"Let's try to make it to the park. Maybe we can get some sleep there. We'll need to keep out of sight though. I suspect there's a no loitering rule there as well."

Under the dim street lights the two made their way to the city park.

After walking about, Sally stopped and slumped down to the ground.

"I can't go any further. Can we just sleep here, on the ground?"

Hershel turned back and moved closer to her.

"No, Sally, we need to get out of sight. If that patrolman catches us, we may very well end up sleeping in a jail cell."

Sally grunted.

Hershel reached down and with some difficulty picked up most of her baggage.

"Come on, we'll find a spot soon." He then started walking away, but glanced back to see Sally wearily getting back to her feet.

A short time later, Hershel spotted something.

"Look, over there!"

Sally again struggled to keep up as Hershel moved quickly towards something.

They arrived at a World War One memorial statue, but more importantly, a tank sat not far from the statue. On the other side of that was a large artillery gun. But, Hershel made his way straight to the tank.

"It's a British Mark Five." Hershel said as he began walking around it.

"A what?" Sally asked.

A British Mark Five tank. During the first world war, we didn't have our own tanks, so we got them from the British or French."

"I'm too tired for a history lesson right now. Can you please look at the tank tomorrow?"

"Look," Hershel pointed at an opening on the side of the tank and behind one of the large guns.

"We have some of this stuff in St. Louis and they let the kids play on it. They've taken the hatch door off this one so the kids can play in it. Maybe we can get some sleep inside."

Sally stared at Hershel as he peeked into the tank.

"Are you serious? Sleep in a tank?"

He glanced back to her. "Would you rather sleep on the ground?"

She moaned and then let out a breath in exasperation.

"Well, let's go in then. I'm too tired to walk any farther."

Hershel nodded and taking their things, climbed into the vehicle.

Soon Sally was climbing in as well. The faint smell of axle grease and motor fuel greeted her.

Hershel found the flashlight and covering most of it with his hand, shined a small light around for them to get situated.

Sally found a place to lay down and using her blouse full of clothes as a pillow was soon trying to get back to sleep.

Hershel also found a place in the corner and after squirming about some, got as comfortable as could be expected in a tank. A short time later they were both asleep.

It was a restless night on the hard, cold floor of the army tank. The two awoke in the morning to sounds of the kitten meowing and a young boy staring at them.

"You got a cat in there?" The boy pointed to the wicker case as Hershel and Sally sleepily sat up.

"Uhm, yeah, well it's actually a kitten." Hershel said.

"Can I see it?" The boy asked as Sally stretched and grimaced with pain.

"Oww, my back." She said, and then reached around to massage it.

"Where do you live? Do you live in here?" The boy asked.

"We, well," Hershel glanced at Sally.

"We're going home now and we really need to get on the way. Maybe you can see the kitten next time; alright?" Sally then began gathering her stuff together, as did Hershel.

"So why did you sleep here?" The boy asked as he stepped aside to give Sally room to move.

"We, just got tired and thought we would take a nap here." Hershel replied

As Sally and Hershel moved towards the hatch, the young boy climbed out of the tank, followed by Sally and then Hershel.

Once outside, the boy persisted. "Don't you have any family? You could take a nap at their house."

Just as Sally was about to reply, a woman that appeared to be the boy's mother came close.

"Charlie, come over here son... hurry up!"

She waved towards the young boy and expressed some concern at the sight of Sally and Hershel having climbed out of the tank; carrying what appeared to be tramp luggage.

As the young boy moved to his mother, Sally brushed some hair from her face and attempted a reply.

"It's uhm... it's our weekend getaway spot... Charlie is welcome to visit anytime though."

The woman grimaced and taking Charlie under her arm, walked away quickly.

A short time later, the two were sitting in a cafe, drinking coffee and sharing an order of toast.

"We're going to have to stay in a motel tonight. My back is killing me. Plus we need to wash some clothes, and I need a bath." Sally then took a drink of her coffee.

"We could get one room and save six dollars." Hershel suggested.

"I told you, that's not proper." She quickly replied.

"I'll sleep on the floor, Sally, I promise you, I won't try anything. We've been traveling together long enough that you should know that."

Sally's face twisted a little as she stared at Hershel.

"Sally, we slept together in a tank last night. What's the difference?"

Now she almost shouted, "We didn't sleep together, Hershel!!"

The cafe became silent and everyone turned to look at the two.

Hershel nodded to Sally, who continued to stare at him, seeming unaware of the attention.

"That's not what I meant. I meant, we've slept in a barn, on the porch of a church and in a tank... If I was going to try anything, I had the opportunity those times. I'm not going to try anything, Sally I swear. We can save some money and still get cleaned up and wash our clothes."

Her face softened some but still had the expression of frustration.

"Well, maybe, but you're going to swear on the Bible once we get a room."

"I will, Sally."

They finished their breakfast and were soon walking along the highway in a dusty, dry heat.

Hershel struggled with his baggage. Sally stopped and turned around. Holding the kitten in her hand, she watched as he shifted the case with his grandmothers ashes from one hand to the other. She shook her head with frustration.

"Hershel..."

"What?" he asked as he came up to her.

"Why don't you just bury her here. There's sand everywhere. I'm sure she would understand, under these conditions."

Hershel glanced down at the case holding the urn. He looked back up at Sally.

"I'm not going to do that, Sally. The only reason I'm going to California is to get my grandmother situated where she wanted to be."

"Why? No one is going to know, Hershel. She's not going to know."

He thought about this for a few seconds, then replied, "I'll know."

She gave him a sour look. Then held her thumb out as a car sped by. Once it was past them, she huffed, turned around and started walking again.

Several miles farther down the highway, they lucked into a ride with a truck driver. Once again, this seemed to be due to Sally being an attractive young woman.

Hershel sat listening to the two converse freely as the open window dusted his hair and gave him a bit of relief from the desert conditions outside.

Later that afternoon, the two were let off in Moriarty, as the truck driver stated he was turning north from there.

The sun was setting low in the sky as they wearily made their way to what looked to be the only motel in town.

After checking in, Hershel walked to a cafe and ordered a hamburger to go, while Sally got cleaned up.

They split the hamburger and then Hershel got cleaned up. Afterwards, the two stayed up until ten o'clock washing their clothes and hanging them about the room.

The following day, they fanned their damp laundry until right before checkout time, in an effort to get it dry.

Then, once again they trudged down the dusty highway with Hershel holding clothes in the air, trying to catch the breeze.

As they came to the outskirts of Moriarty, they passed a novelty "Gypsy Fortune Teller" sign.

Unexpectedly, a woman from the house beside the sign, called out to them.

"You two, hello. Could you spare a few minutes?"

Hershel and Sally stopped. Turning to the woman, they noticed she was dressed in what could only be described as an elaborate and colorful gypsy costume.

She waved at them from the porch in an effort move them to the house.

Sally glanced at Hershel. He shrugged his shoulders and nodded very slightly. The two then moved slowly towards the extravagantly decorated house.

"Hurry, come inside." the woman said, still motioning to them with her hand.

They stepped onto the porch of the old two story house, which was painted an off green color with black trim.

The screen door squeaked as they proceeded inside. Following the strangely dressed woman they soon found themselves in a dimly lit room. In the middle sat a round table and sitting in the middle of the table was crystal ball.

"Sit down, please." The woman motioned to them.

"Uhm, we were just.."

"Shhh....shh... don't speak. I don't want to know anything about either one of you." The woman said.

After they all had a seat, the woman closed her eyes and began humming out loud. Then she raised her hands into the air, and after lowering them she opened her eyes and began to study the crystal ball.

"I see it, I see... the gray Albatross has flown into the sky. The clouds are dark..." Her eyes then grew wide as she appeared to be in slight pain.

"Oh my, oh dear..."

"What? what is it?" Sally asked.

"Billy the Kid rides again!" The woman looked at Sally with a crazy expression; then focused her attention back on the crystal ball.

"I see two buttercups floating on a marmalade sea of mystery."

Sally now glanced at Hershel. Her eyes expressed confusion and a slight bit of fear.

The woman continued. "Here, there and everywhere. The sea's are rough but the two buttercups stay afloat!

"Now, there's a mangled mass of metal... oh my goodness, the dogs of war are relentless and tweetie is almost eaten alive!"

The woman then became even more excited, "There's more! The mighty hawk takes the two buttercups on a flight into the skies. Then," she looked even closer into the ball and continued. "Then, the two buttercups land safely on shore and.... BINGO!!" She shouted, causing Sally to jump.

The room suddenly became quiet. The woman brushed her brow as if removing perspiration. She looked at her two startled guests and expelled a breath of air.

"I've still got it!" She said, seeming relieved.

Hershel and Sally stared at her, but remained silent.

"Oh and there won't be any charge for that. I just wanted to make sure I wasn't getting rusty."

Sally glanced at Hershel. He smiled slightly and said, "Uhmm, thank you?"

Seeming to relax some, Sally asked, "What, uh, well, what does it mean?"

The woman glanced at Sally and smiled, "I have no idea, it's your fortune. It has something to do with your past or future, or both. But, the bingo part sounds very good. If I were you, I would be excited about that, if nothing else."

Sally's faced again twisted into a puzzled expression.

"Would you two like some tea?"

Hershel looked at the damp laundry he still held in his arms.

"Do you have a place we could hang these to dry?"

The woman glanced at the clothes. "Oh, certainly. You can hang them on the porch while we have our tea."

A few minutes later, the laundry was hanging over the porch railing. Hershel and Sally sat down in some weathered chairs to wait for the woman.

"Do, you really think this was a good idea? This woman seems to have a few screws lose." Sally then leaned over to glance into the screen door, as if to be sure the woman was not close.

Hershel also glanced into the screen, then replied, "The way I see it, we'll have a chance to let our clothes dry. Plus, it's been too long since I've had a good cup of tea."

Sally stared at Hershel for several seconds.

"Why am I suddenly thinking about Tex?"

Hershel's head twisted a bit. "I don't know; do you miss him?"

Sally squinted, as if trying to grab a thought from the air.

"What? no, of course not. I, don't know... It was something you said." She replied.

Then the woman came out carrying a tray with the tea.

"I'm sorry that we've not been properly introduced. My name is Maud, by the way." She then sat the tray down and glanced up to her guests.

"Hershel."

"Sally."

The woman smiled and nodded, then began pouring the tea.

Once they all had their drinks, along with some sugar and a bit of cream for Hershel, they relaxed in their chairs.

"So, have you lived here all your life, Maud?" Sally asked.

"No, I'm originally from Tennessee. I was on my way out to California when my car broke down."

"That's where we're headed, " Hershel said.

"Really? what do you plan to do out there?"

"I've got, well, some business to take care of for my grandmother. But Sally is planning on being an actress."

The woman got excited, "Well, I was planning on getting into acting myself." She then exhaled a breath and glanced out over the porch, as if recalling memories.

"But, I broke down here. Then I got a job at the cafe and well, it just never worked out. I did mange to buy this place though. And, the fact that I can tell fortunes has helped."

Sally glanced over to Hershel, then took a drink of her tea.

An hour and several cups of tea later, the two travelers gathered their dry laundry up and said good-bye to Maud.

"Well, she was real nice. And, makes great tea."

Sally nodded a little, "yeah, I suppose she wasn't as crazy as I thought."

The two walked several miles out of town and caught a ride that carried them to the west side of Albuquerque. With daylight swiftly diminishing, they once again got something to eat and checked into a motel.

As Hershel got comfortable on the floor, Sally counted her money.

"Something has to happen. We're almost broke."

Hershel grunted.

"Did you hear me, Hershel?"

"Yeah, I heard you. But, it's not going to help getting worked up about it. I'm sure something will come up."

Sally huffed a bit, then folded up her money, put it up and turned off the lamp.

The following morning, they refilled their bottles with water and after a light meal and coffee, were back on the highway.

"I can't wait to see the Grand Canyon!" Hershel exclaimed as both held their thumbs out for a passing truck.

The breeze from the vehicle pelted the two with a sandy heat.

"We're down to our last few dollars, and you're thinking about the Grand Canyon? What are we supposed to eat, cactus?"

"You worry too much, Sally. Something will come up."

She gave him a disgruntled stare. But then her expression softened some.

"I don't think you worry enough," she replied, as they turned and again trudged westward.

Several rides and many miles later, the two were let off at an intersection in Gallup New Mexico. The sun was dropping to the horizon as they spotted a bus station sign and made their way towards it.

"I hope we don't get ran off from this one," Sally commented as they came closer.

"It looks like the restrooms are on the side of the station. Maybe if we don't have to go in, we won't attract any attention." Hershel said wearily.

They cleaned up some and sat on a bench outside the station.

"Give me Mitsy," Sally said.

Hershel looked at her with a puzzled expression.

"Mitsy? you mean the kitten?"

"Yeah, the kitten."

"So, you named her Mitsy?" Hershel asked as he opened the wicker case.

"Yes, I named her, she's got to have a name."

Hershel smiled, but not where Sally could see it.

Once Sally had Mitsy and began feeding her, Hershel asked, "so... where did you come up with 'Mitsy'?"

Sally smiled a little as the kitten ate a leftover French fry.

"Oh, I just like the name. And, I always thought, if I had a cat, I would name it Mitsy."

Hershel continued to watch her feeding the kitten. It was now very dark other than a single street light.

"So, you've never had a cat of your own?"

"No, my folks weren't much of what you would call "pet" people. I always wanted one when I was a kid, but I finally gave up on ever getting one."

"Well, now you have one. And I like the name Mitsy. I think it fits her." Hershel said.

Sally looked at him and they both smiled. Later they slept restlessly, but otherwise undisturbed through the night.

Heavy exhaust fumes from a noisy bus roused the two early the next morning.

Both spent several minutes stretching and trying to work out the soreness from sleeping on the hard bench.

As they split an order of toast in the small bus station cafe, Sally once again thumbed through the few dollars they had left.

"We've got a long stretch coming up. I don't see how we're going to get across it."

Hershel considered this as he finished his coffee and held the cup up for the waitress to see. Soon she brought the coffee pot and refilled it.

"We could look around here for some work. Maybe there's a church that could put us up until we earned a pay check."

Sally glanced at him. She expressed a bit of fright.

Shaking her head she finally replied. "I don't know. I don't want to end up like Maud. I'm afraid if I stop, I'll never get started again."

Hershel stared at Sally for several seconds as she slipped a small piece of toast to Mitsy.

"Well, Sally, I'm going to California. I'm not afraid. I have a mission to get my grandmother settled. We'll find a way."

She looked at him and then a subtle smile broke over her face.

"I'm glad one of us is so sure."

Chapter Nine: A Skinny Deal

Once again they set out in the dusty heat. Several miles outside of Gallup they caught a ride with a rancher. The old pick-up rumbled slowly along.

They were let out at what seemed to be the middle of nowhere. They thanked the rancher and he then turned and drove up a dirt road towards what Hershel thought must be his ranch.

They began walking west. An hour passed and they were still walking. Several vehicles passed by but none stopped. They continued in the heat of the day.

"I can't take this much longer. I wish we would get a ride, this is ridiculous." Sally stumbled along several yards behind Hershel.

He glanced back to her, adjusted the footstool over his shoulder and then turned back west.

"Hey, what's that?"

Sally looked up and far in the distance, she could see a structure of some type.

"I don't know, but it's a long ways away." She then expelled a breath of air in an exhausted manner.

Hershel went back to her and took the blouse that she had fashioned into a bag. He hung the blouse bag over his arm, as she shifted her other burdens around to a more comfortable position.

They walked another hour and finally came close enough for Hershel to identify a "Texaco" sign. Another fifteen minutes of walking brought them up to a gas station with a small store, and beside it sat a large salvage yard with hundreds of derelict cars and trucks.

A sign over the entrance of the salvage yard read "Skinny's Auto Salvage."

Once they were in front of the old store, they saw a man sitting on the porch with a cigar in his mouth. He was a hefty man, in his late forties or early fifties. He had overalls on, a somewhat rough appearance and looked like a mechanic.

"You two are traveling in some hot weather." The man said as they noticed him.

"Yes Sir, we are that." Hershel replied.

They stood under the hot sun for several seconds, then Sally pulled Hershel's arm to move him closer.

In almost a whisper, she said, "ask him if he has any work we could do."

Hershel nodded and then turned to the man.

"Uhm, would you happened to have any work we could do, to earn some money. We're headed to California, and due to some, uhm, unforeseen events, we're in a tight situation financially."

"Is that so? Well, that's too bad. In a tight situation you say." The man reached over and took a box of matches from a table. He re-lit the cigar and pulled a couple of draws from it.

"You two come on up here and sit a while. I'll give it some thought."

They both eagerly stepped up and under the shade of the porch.

The man leaned over and yelled through the screen door of the store, "Erma!"

Soon a woman in what appeared to be a home sewn dress came out. She was around the same age of the man and wore a time weathered apron around her waist.

"This is my wife Erma," The man said.

The woman nodded and smiling said, "hello."

"Hi, I'm Sally and this is Hershel."

The man then turned to Erma, "Could we get a glass of tea for these two young folks."

Erma nodded and went back into the store.

"You can just call me Skinny. This is my station and that's my salvage yard. The Missus takes care of the store."

Skinny pulled another draw from his cigar. He looked at Hershel and then Sally. He glanced back at Hershel and then back to

Sally. Hershel noticed he studied her very closely. Then he continued.

"I ain't hiring right now. But perhaps we could work something out. I hate to see young folks in a tight situation."

Erma came out with three glasses and a pitcher of tea. Each glass had a few ice cubes in it. She poured the tea and handed each one a glass.

"You wouldn't happen to be a mechanic, would you Hershel?"

Hershel was taking a drink of the tea, but lowered the glass and replied, "no Sir, I'm afraid not. But I am a fast learner."

"Hmm, well, that makes it a bit more difficult." Skinny said.

He then looked out into the sky, over Hershel and Sally, as if considering the situation. He took a drink of his tea and sat the glass back on the table.

"I do have a number of cars and trucks that I was planning on changing out the motors or transmissions, so that I could sell them." he paused. "But, that would take several weeks at least. You two got a place to stay?"

Hershel and Sally glanced at each other, then Hershel answered, "No, Sir. We don't have a place to stay."

Skinny took in a large breath, and then exhaled as he seemed to study Sally again.

"Well, I do have a place out back. It's where me and the Missus stayed before we bought this store from my uncle. It's not much though."

Sally nudged Hershel with her elbow and he quickly spoke up.

"We don't need much, Sir, just enough to get by until we can earn some money."

Skinny cleared his throat, "well, that's the thing. I wouldn't be able to pay you much. What I was thinking was perhaps working out a trade. If you help get these cars of mine running, so that I can sell them, then I'll fix you two up with some transportation. You'll have to change the motor out and get it running. But, you can use my tools and do it in your spare time."

Hershel glanced at Sally. She had no expression on her face. But then she spoke up.

"By, not paying much, just how much are you talking about?"

Skinny looked off into the clouds and appeared to be doing math in his mind. Finally he replied.

"Hmm, well, I'll be providing your living quarters. And I'll have to do some training before Hershel will be much help... but, I think I could afford a dollar a day, that is if Hershel learns quickly."

Hershel felt Sally stiffen up. She then took his arm.

"Could you let us talk it over, Skinny?" She then pulled Hershel up and down the two steps of the porch.

When they were out of earshot, she spoke with a muffled voice.

"A dollar a day? He's trying to take advantage of us!"

Hershel glanced back to Skinny, who sat smoking his cigar.

"Well, the way I see it, we don't have much of a choice, Sally."

"You've got to negotiate, Hershel, that's almost nothing!"

"Yeah, but, if we get a car, we can drive to California, and sleep in the car. We won't have to get a motel room, at least not as often. We should be able to save enough for gas to get us past the Grand Canyon, at least."

Sally's mouth twisted as she considered this.

"That's true. But I don't like the dollar a day deal. You've got to try and get more."

"Alright, I'll try."

She nodded and they went back to the porch.

After sitting back down, Hershel said, "A dollar a day isn't much, Skinny. If you could raise that some we might have a deal."

Skinny smiled, "Oh, well, I thought you two were in a tight situation. You see, I'm not in a tight situation for help. I just thought we might work something out that would be mutually beneficial... I'm afraid that's the deal, take it or leave it."

The two watched him for several seconds as he puffed his cigar and then took a drink of tea.

Hershel looked over to Sally. She had a grim expression, but finally said, "we'll take it."

Skinny perked up, "good, I'm glad we can help each other out."

He then directed the two over to his salvage yard.

Soon after entering the fenced in area, dogs started barking. Hershel could see at least six large dogs chained up in several areas. Some were chained to old cars that they also appeared to be using for a dog house. Others were connected to stakes in the ground and had ramshackle dog houses to sleep in.

"Here now!! Quiet! it's just me!" Skinny shouted out, and the dogs hushed somewhat, but still barked occasionally, as if unsure about Hershel and Sally.

"Them's my watch dogs. They keep the thieves out." Skinny then took out a slug of tobacco and bit off a piece as they continued towards the back of the yard.

"You got a problem with thieves?" Hershel asked as they moved along a trail in-between derelict cars with doors and various parts missing from their bodies.

"No, I don't have a problem with 'em, 'cause I've got guard dogs!" Skinny then turned his head and spat some of the dark colored tobacco juice out.

They continued a bit farther and Skinny raised his hand to point, "There she is!"

He brought attention to a very old and weathered bus, that had obviously been converted into living quarters.

"Great, another bus." Sally said.

"Hmmm?" Skinny asked her.

"Oh, I said..., great! It's a bus!"

Suddenly, two large dogs came from separate directions at full speed, barking viciously.

Sally let out a scream and stepped back. Hershel also stepped back as the dogs hit the end of their chains, but still snapped and barked at the two.

"Here now! Hush you two!" Skinny shouted and the two dogs backed down a bit.

Skinny, then started walking along a trail leading to the bus.

"As long as you stay on the trail, you'll be alright." He said.

When Sally and Hershel followed behind, the two dogs rushed again and barked incessantly, paying particular attention to the wicker case that Hershel carried.

Sally was obviously apprehensive and squealed a bit as she moved to avoid the dogs. Though they barked viciously, they could not quiet reach the trail due to the length of their chains.

Arriving at the bus, which sat in a small hollow, Skinny took in a deep breath, as if reminiscing his time living there.

Hershel gazed around, as the dogs continued to bark behind them. He noticed a variety of dilapidated yard ornaments scattered about and some plant pots, of which only dried dirt remained in them.

Looking over the bus, it appeared to be thirty years old, at least. He saw that the wheels had been removed and the bus sat flat on the ground. Pieces of tin were placed in the wheel wells to hide the bare axles. A coat of white paint had long turned to a faded tan color and in places Hershel noticed yellow splotches, which indicated this to have been a school bus at one time.

"There she is. It's not the Ritz, but it has all the comforts of home." Skinny then turn to Hershel. "I'm guessing you two are married."

Sally stood on the other side of Skinny, where Hershel noticed an immediate expression of shock and fright come over her face.

Hershel felt flush from the sudden comment by Skinny. His mind raced.

"You... uhh, you sure guess good, Skinny." Sally replied from behind.

Skinny turned and examined her briefly, then took a couple of steps and spat on the ground.

Behind him, Sally still had a frightened expression. But as Skinny moved and opened the door of the bus, her expression relaxed and she even smiled a bit.

As Skinny walked up the steps of the bus, he continued.

"It's got running water, a cook stove, refrigerator, bathroom in the back and electricity... well, enough to power the fridge, a few lights and a radio anyhow."

The inside was cramped at best. Hershel and Sally examined it as they stood behind Skinny.

Over the windows were homemade curtains. There was a small cook stove, sink, refrigerator and couch towards the middle. To the rear of the bus was a full size bed and homemade curtains, strategically placed to provide privacy. In the back corner was a small room that appeared to be the bathroom.

After stepping back out of the bus, Skinny said, "I hope you two will be comfortable. We'll get started first thing in the morning, Hershel. I'll tell you what, I'll even throw in your lunch, how does that sound?"

"That sounds very good, Sir. I'll be ready first thing in the morning."

Skinny nodded and made his way back towards the store as Hershel and Sally went back into the bus.

Once inside, Sally plopped down on the couch, then looked around the bus with a concerned expression.

"I don't know about this. I mean, this is not much better than camping out."

Hershel moved over and opened the small refrigerator. After glancing in to see it was empty, he replied, "Well, it's better than sleeping in a tank."

Sally laughed a little at this comment. She reached down, opened the wicker case, then the small wooden box to retrieve Mitsy.

As the kitten purred in her lap, she continued, "I suppose you're right. But we'll really have to watch our money. It's good that Skinny will be providing your lunch. If we save every dime, we might have enough to get to California... or the state line at least."

She then stood up and examined the small sink beside the stove. "Everything's going to need cleaned. It doesn't look this place has been lived in for a while. I may as well get started."

As Sally cleaned the kitchen area, Mitsy played around her feet. Hershel began cleaning in the small bathroom.

He called Sally in, to look at the "shower head," which was a water pipe sticking out of the wall and a tin can with holes in it, attached to the pipe. They both laughed and then returned to their tasks.

The following morning, Hershel was stirred from sleep by the many dogs barking. He sat up from his bed on the couch, then glanced out a window and noticed Skinny in the distance, mulling around the salvage yard.

Hershel ate a light breakfast and dodging the two dogs stationed around the front of the bus. He met Skinny by what appeared to be a homemade hoist used for pulling motors from cars. There were two, cut off telephone poles, embedded into the ground and standing about ten feet high. On top of these, a section of railroad track was secured and in the middle were chains and a large pulley device.

Around this was an open bay area built of tin and two-by-fours. This it seemed, was built to provide shade and cover for anyone working around the makeshift engine hoist. The entire area smelled of oil, gasoline and axle grease.

"Morning Hershel. Are you ready to get started?"

"Good morning Skinny. I'm ready."

With this greeting began Hershel's dive into the world of auto mechanics. Skinny pointed out what car to start on. Hershel would hook the vehicle up to the wench truck and Skinny would tow it to the work area.

Then Skinny pointed at what to do next, and next. Hershel soon realized, the only thing Skinny was planning to do was point and tell him what needed done.

Around lunch time, Skinny opened his lunch box and took out two boloney sandwiches. One for him and one for Hershel. Along with a glass of tea, that would be the extent of the "provided," lunch.

The following day, Sally caught Hershel before he left the bus.

128

"Hershel, ask Skinny if he has some thin rope or something that we can run for a clothes line. I can wash some clothes in the sink, but I need somewhere to hang them."

He nodded and then left for work.

When asked about the clothes line at lunch time, Skinny rubbed his chin while in thought. He glanced down towards the bus.

"I can put the line up, Skinny. We just need some cable or even a thin rope."

"Oh, that's fine Hershel. I've got some cable somewhere. I'll put the line up for you. I've got a spot in mind that'll work well."

This immediately struck Hershel as being odd, since Skinny seemed reluctant to do anything other than direct the labor of his new mechanic in training.

Nevertheless, Hershel thanked him and thought little about it until that evening when he told Sally.

"That's great, we need some clothes washed soon. Neither one of us has much to wear."

The following morning, as Hershel carefully dodged the two dogs beside the trail, he noticed Skinny securing a long line between two derelict trucks.

The cable was around forty feet in length and stood around five feet from the ground. As Hershel came closer, Skinny finished tightening the turn buckles that secured the cable.

"There you are. A clothes line for Sally. You can let her know it's ready to go." Skinny then smiled, turned and spat a stream of tobacco juice on the ground.

"Well, ahh, thanks Skinny. It's a bit far from the bus though, don't you think?"

Skinny glanced up to the work area used for pulling motors, which was in clear view from the clothes line. He then looked back to Hershel.

"No, no, this is the best spot. Lots of sun and a good breeze for drying your clothes."

Hershel nodded. "Oh, alright. Well, I'll go tell Sally, she'll be glad to know it's ready."

Upon hearing the news and then looking out the window to spot the clothes line, Sally became upset.

"Why did he put it out there? I'll have to go past those stupid dogs every time I hang clothes!"

"I said something about it being too far. He said there was a lot of sun and a breeze to dry the clothes."

Sally grunted and then put the plug in the sink and started running some water.

"Oh, whatever. At least I can get some clothes washed."

Hershel left to start work with Skinny.

Later, Hershel had his head under the hood of a late, nineteen thirties model Ford. Skinny sat on a stool smoking a cigar while pointing out the "manifold" bolts that needed removed.

The dogs in front of the bus began to bark very aggressively, and soon Hershel heard Sally let out a short scream.

Pulling his head out from under the hood, he spotted her in a tug of war with one of the dogs that had latched onto a piece of clothing. Sally pulled on what looked to be one of Hershel's shirts, as the dog growled and shook it's head.

Meanwhile the other dog jerked at the end of its chain in an effort to get a bite on Sally's behind, of which was facing the dog.

Sally struggled desperately to get the shirt back and still not get a bite on her rear section.

Hershel glanced over to Skinny, who was puffing on his cigar and smiling; seeming quite entertained by the spectacle.

Sally finally managed to pull the now ripped shirt from the dog's grasp, then hopped and skipped out of harms way and on to the clothes line.

Hershel returned to his task under the hood of the car, but glancing up from time to time, noticed that Skinny was, very closely, watching Sally hang the laundry.

130

Then, the dogs began barking again and Hershel moved from the car to see Sally once more dodge through the gauntlet of the two guard dogs.

Skinny chuckled a little as Sally swerved from one side to the other and let out a slight squeal.

"Maybe Sally could make friends with the dogs?" Hershel suggested.

"Well... maybe she could." Skinny replied, once Sally was back in the bus.

"What's their names?"

"The Black and tan one on the right is named Blackie. The tan and black one on the left is named Brownie." Skinny then puffed on his cigar that had almost gone out.

That evening, Hershel stepped wearily into the old bus.

"It's almost nine o'clock!" Sally said.

Hershel plopped down on the couch. "Yeah, I know. Is there anything to eat?"

"Yeah, I bought some soup. But I'm telling you, the prices in Skinny's store are outrageous. It's going to be hard to save any money at the rate he's paying you and with what we'll need to spend in his store for food." She pulled a spoon from a small dish drainer. "And, Erma is not very sociable. I could hardly get a word out of her. She's nice and all, but defiantly not one for conversation."

She lit the burner under a pan that she found in a cabinet of the bus.

"I'll get cleaned up." Hershel then took his pair of swimming trunks and a shirt from the folded clothes Sally had washed.

Lifting the shirt up he saw it was ripped from playing tug-of-war with Blackie.

Sally had begun stirring the soup but raised her hand to the shirt as Hershel studied it.

"And that's another thing! You need to ask Skinny if we can move that clothes line. Those stupid dogs, they just hate me... I guess."

Hershel glanced at Sally as she returned her attention to the soup.

"I can ask him, Sally, but I think he's fairly satisfied with where it's at now."

She turned to him, "why? why does it have to be there?"

"Oh, I think it's just.. out in the open... in the sunshine and clear view. You know, breezy and all that."

Sally looked at him, seeming puzzled by his answer.

"That doesn't make much sense. I don't see any difference between close to the bus and way out there."

Hershel winced a little, but then replied, "No, but I'm pretty sure he can see a difference."

Sally huffed a bit as she continued to stir the soup.

"Well, he's taking advantage of you. Is he going to work you twelve hours a day, every day?"

Hershel walked into the small bathroom and shut the thin door.

"I suppose he might. But, we don't have much choice as far as I see it. If we can get this car he's talking about, then we'll save money and not have to hitch hike to California. I think we need to stick it out. I don't mind the work and he is teaching me how to repair cars. That's a plus."

Sally mumbled something that he didn't understand. He got cleaned up and ate some of the soup. Then laid down on the couch and went directly to sleep.

For two weeks straight the routine continued in this manner. Hershel worked from sun up till sun down everyday, except Sunday.

Sally continued to lose battles of tug-of-war with their laundry. Blackie and Brownie went to great efforts in order to catch a piece of the laundry she carried and then tear it up as completely as possible.

Although Sally borrowed needle and thread from Erma in order to mend their clothes; what little they had to wear was slowly becoming "beyond repair," as Sally put it one day.

On a particularly sunny day, Hershel was rebuilding a carburetor to be installed on one of the cars that Skinny planned to sell. Skinny sat on his stool, chewing his tobacco on this occasion, rather than smoking a cigar.

As he watched Sally once again in a tussle with the dogs over her laundry, he asked, "does Sally smell like a cat?"

Hershel stopped working on the carburetor.

He turned and watched Sally as she moved to and fro, soldiering-on in her struggle with Brownie and Blackie. It appeared that Brownie had the upper hand on a pair of her Capri pants and Sally was putting forth a great effort to win them back, without getting a nip on her behind from Blackie.

"I, uhm... well, I'm not real sure what a cat smells like, Skinny. Why do you ask?"

Skinny spat on the ground and then turned back to the laundry battle. Sally screamed a bit and then squealed, but managed to pull the Capri's from Brownie and then quickly retreated towards the bus.

"Them dogs hate cats. They act like she's a cat or something. It's real strange. Seems apparent she's had no luck making friends with 'em."

Hershel picked up a grease rag and wiped off his wrench. He cleared his throat and replied, "no, she tried calling them by name and even made a peace offering; one slice of baloney for each. But, they don't seem to be interested in a truce."

He then picked up the carburetor and returned to his task of rebuilding it.

When Hershel came in that evening, Sally appeared to still be upset from her confrontation with the dogs.

"Did he say anything about the car today?"

Hershel took the plate of food she handed him and sat down on the couch.

"He said that he has one picked out and he'll show it to me this week. Maybe I can start working on it Sunday."

Sally huffed as she picked up Mitsy and started petting her.

"It won't be soon enough, I can tell you that."

Hershel took a drink of water. He looked at Sally. She still had a frustrated expression.

"I'm just now to where I can work on it, Sally. So far, I've rebuilt four generators. Three carburetors. One complete engine overhaul and two transmission rebuilds. Plus several engine and transmission pulls and reinstalls. So, I'm feeling like I can start working on it, but last week I wouldn't have had the same amount of confidence."

She walked over and picked up the Capri's, displaying the extensive damage from the tug-of-war with Brownie.

"Well, I'm telling you, we won't have anything to wear by the time we do get away from here!"

Hershel glanced at the Capri's and nodded as he chewed his food.

"I can't fix these... I'll have to make shorts out of them. It's the only way to salvage anything." She then tossed them on the end of the couch and went back to petting Mitsy.

Later that week, Skinny took Hershel to a corner of the salvage yard and pointed out a well worn and weathered 1931 Dodge sedan. They then walked to another part of the yard and Skinny showed him a Dodge pickup that had extensive damage to the bed. He told Hershel a large tree had fallen on the truck, but the motor was still good and would fit in the sedan.

That evening as the sun was setting on the horizon, Hershel took Sally and showed her the car.

"That? Are you serious? It looks like it's completely worn out!"

She glanced inside. "The seats are in bad shape, and the headliner is falling down! I can't believe it. You've been working sun up till sun down for almost a month and he gives us this...thing!"

Hershel motioned with his hands in an effort to calm her.

"Sally, it's not much, but if I can get it running, it just needs to get us to California. And, we can sleep in it; we can, maybe do some odd jobs along the way. That way we won't need to get a motel room."

He stepped back and watched her closely. She calmed down some and appeared to be thinking it over.

"I guess we can get cleaned up at service station restrooms." She again looked the car over with an expression of disappointment.

134

But then continued. "Maybe I can wash a few clothes each time we stop for gas. That is, if we have any clothes left by then."

Hershel smiled. "Yeah, that's right. It'll work out, Sally. You'll see."

As Sunday approached, Hershel labored under the hood of a car, but heard Blackie and Brownie barking once again; indicating Sally was entering their territory.

Skinny had been watching Hershel from his standard spot on a stool. He was drinking a glass of tea, but perked up and turned to watch Sally when the dogs started barking.

"Well, it looks like Sally got her some new clothes." Skinny said with enthusiasm.

Hershel stepped back from under the hood and looked at Sally, who had by now made it past Blackie and Brownie. She had her back to Hershel and Skinny and was beginning to hang clothes on the line.

"Oh, no those aren't new. They were actually a pair of pants that she cut off to make shorts out of, after Brownie got hold of them." Hershel then went back under the hood.

"She's been reluctant to wear them because she had to cut them off shorter than what she wanted to."

Skinny continued to watch Sally but said, "Oh, I think they're fine. She shouldn't worry herself about that."

After a few more minutes, Skinny casually asked, "Have you ever had to give Sally a spanking?"

Hershel raised up quickly and bumped his head on the hood.

"Oww..." He rubbed his head and looked at Skinny, who had never turned his attention from Sally.

"Why would I do something like that?" He asked, still rubbing his head and moving out from under the hood.

Skinny glanced at Hershel, but quickly turned back to Sally.

"Oh, you know... some women need a spanking now and then."

Hershel stopped rubbing his head, but examined Skinny for a few seconds, to be sure he wasn't joking.

"Really?" he finally asked.

"Sure," Skinny said. he took another drink of tea and continued. "And, there's some women that actually want a spanking from time to time."

Hershel's face became a bit twisted as he considered this.

"Are you pulling my leg, Skinny?"

Somewhat reluctantly, Skinny turned from the sight of Sally hanging clothes.

"Not at all. In fact, from my studies of the fairer sex over the years, I've discovered there are women that need a spanking from time to time. And, there are women that want a spanking ever now and then. But, the real prizes are the ones that need one and want one from time to time. Them are the best kind of women."

He straightened up a bit and continued.

"I'll tell you what, Hershel. The next time Sally gives you any trouble, you just ask her if she needs a spanking. You'll know right away what you've got. I'm thinking you might get lucky and find out she's the best kind."

Hershel glanced back out to Sally, who was now dodging the dogs again in order to make it to the bus, in one piece.

"Uhh, alright, I'll keep that in mind. And, thanks Skinny."

Skinny nodded and smiled. Hershel returned to his labors under the hood of the car.

Saturday afternoon, Skinny helped Hershel pull the old Dodge sedan up to the hoist area, in order for him to begin removing the motor.

The next day Hershel got up early and began working on the car. Sally brought him lunch and watched for a while.

"You're really pretty good at this stuff," she commented as he worked.

"Yeah, I kind of like this sort of work. I always took care of my grandmother and never really learned any type of skill or trade."

Sally sat on the stool that Skinny normally sat on. After watching a bit more, she replied.

136

"It seems Skinny is giving you the fast track education in auto mechanics."

Hershel laughed as he connected chains to the old motor.

"I suppose so. But, he really does know his stuff. I feel fortunate to be learning from him. And, the fact that I've had to do all the work means I've also had to learn quickly."

Sally smiled. "You really are the eternal optimist aren't you, Hershel?"

The following Sunday Hershel had the old pick-up under the hoist and soon had the motor out.

Two weeks later, Hershel loaded the last of their luggage into the old Dodge. He got in, started it up and pulled it over to the fuel pump. After filling it up, along with two, beat up Army surplus gas cans that Skinny had given them, he went into the store and found Sally talking to Erma.

"And thanks so much for everything," she said.

"You're very welcome Sally, and I hope you two have a safe trip to California."

"Have you seen Skinny?" Hershel asked.

"He went out back; said he had one more thing for you." Erma said.

"Well, the gas and bonus was quite a surprise. He doesn't need to do anything else." When Hershel said this, Sally gave him a sour look.

"But, we'll sure be grateful. Anything at all will be helpful right now."

They said good-bye to Erma and were soon waiting in the Dodge for Skinny.

"With the free gas and the 'very' small bonus he gave you, we have sixty three dollars. Plus a few groceries that Erma pitched in. It's going to be tight, but we might make it."

Hershel nodded to Sally and then noticed Skinny walking up to them carrying a basket.

"Maybe it's some more food. That would be helpful." Hershel said.

Skinny approached the drivers side door.

"Hershel, you've been a real help. And, you've turned into a fairly decent mechanic. Are you sure you don't want to stay?"

Looking past Skinny, he could see seven cars and two pick-ups sitting in front, all with for sale signs on them. He expelled a breath as he recalled the labor involved with those vehicles.

"Oh, I really appreciate the offer, Skinny. And, I'm really grateful for all you've done and taught me. But, we need to get on our way."

"Well, alright then... I've got one more thing for you two."

He lifted the small basket and handed it through the window.

Once it was inside, Hershel saw that it was a small black and tan puppy.

"Oh, uhm... well you really don't need to do that, Skinny. We know how much you use your dogs around here. But thanks just the same."

Sally's face winced a bit as she glanced into the basket.

"Oh, it's no problem at all, that there is the pick of the litter. There was thirteen pups in that litter. Brownie can put a litter like that out several times a year. No, I insist. You'll need a good guard dog out there in California. I also put a little sack of dog food in the basket. No charge."

Hershel glanced at Sally. She rolled her eyes, but where Skinny couldn't see it.

"Well, uhm, if you insist, Skinny. And thanks again for everything."

Sally put the basket at her feet and then leaned over and gave Skinny a tight lipped smile, seeming reluctant to open her mouth and speak.

Hershel shifted the old car into gear and they were soon rolling down the highway.

"Great, another mouth to feed." She shook her head as the breeze from the windows tossed her hair about.

"Oh, it's not so bad, I think it's kind of cute," Hershel said in a loud voice, in order to be heard over the open windows and old car.

"You would," she replied; prompting a smile from Hershel.

Chapter Ten: Birds of a White Feather

Around twenty miles down the road, they crossed the state line into Arizona. This immediately perked the two up and to Hershel's astonishment, Sally picked up the puppy and looked it over. Then she held it for a while and watched out the window as the arid desert scenery passed by.

For several days, everything went well. They moved through the Grand Canyon, stopping from time to time to get a view.

They would get cleaned up at service stations where they bought gas. Sally would wash a few of their patched up and repaired clothes. Then they would hang them over the seats of the old Dodge and let the breeze dry them as they drove along.

The car wouldn't go very fast, but it was steady. They parked and slept in it and though not comfortable, it didn't cost any of their precious financial reserves. However, twenty miles outside of Kingman Arizona, the car began to have problems.

"Can you fix it?" Sally asked as Hershel avoided the steam from the hot engine.

"It's overheated. We'll have to let it cool down and add some water. Hopefully we can get into Kingman."

Later, Hershel pulled the old sedan into a service station at the edge of the city.

The engine was overheated again and steam bellowed around the hood.

The service attendant came out and the looked it over as Sally went to the restroom.

"I'd say it's your water pump." The attendant said as he gazed over the motor.

"Can we make it to California?" Hershel asked.

"You mean without changing it?"

"Yeah, we're uhm, well a little tight on money right now."

The attendant then seemed to notice the patched and tattered clothing that Hershel wore.

"Well, that's understandable. It happens to ever one."

He turned his attention back to the car; took his hat off and scratched his head. After a few more seconds of thought her replied.

"I don't think it's gone all the way out, from what you've told me. You could try to baby it along; it might make it. The problem is, if it goes out, it's out for good. I ain't ever had much luck rebuilding the pumps on these old Dodges. If I were you, I would get a new one."

At this time, Sally came to the car and started to get in. The attendant examined her patched up clothing and added, "or you could maybe get a used one from a salvage yard."

"By 'baby it along', what do you mean?" Hershel asked.

"Well, you could keep plenty of water with you. I've got some old jugs and bottles around that you can have. I would only drive her forty or fifty miles before letting the engine cool down and then adding some water to the radiator. Keep her from getting overheated again and you might make it."

"The jugs and bottles would help a lot. And I sure thank you." Hershel said.

After filling the radiator with water and then every jug and bottle that could be scrounged up, the two headed back out on the highway.

"Are we going to make it?" Sally asked.

Hershel glanced over at her and couldn't help but smile as she held the puppy on her lap and Mitsy was on her chest; climbing into her hair.

"I hope so. Even if we could find another water pump, I don't have any tools to install it."

They continued west, stopping ever forty miles or so and letting the engine cool down. Then, Hershel would top off the radiator and they would proceed again.

Their progress slowed. That evening they came to some hills and decided to wait until morning to attempt getting over them.

Early the next morning, Hershel searched for a stream or source of water as they came closer to the large hills.

"There's something!"

Slowing down and then stopping, the two looked out at a windmill on the other side of a barbed wire fence. At the bottom of the windmill sat a large round tub that held water, which the windmill pumped up for cattle.

"That's in someone's field, Hershel. You mean to tell me you're going to go over there and take some water?" Sally then turned to Hershel, who still sat studying the windmill outside of Sally's window.

He expelled a long breath of air and answered, "desperate times call for desperate measures. Unless we refill our water jugs, we won't make it over those hills. Who knows where the next source of water is."

Hershel gathered the jugs and bottles, then slipped across the fence. Sally stood on the other side. The windmill squeaked noisily as Hershel filled them, then took each one to Sally and she loaded them in the car.

Once they had everything that could hold water filled and were driving away from the windmill, both laughed out loud.

"I feel like I robbed a bank or something!" Hershel said.

"Oh, I doubt the farmer will miss that little bit of water." Sally replied.

Glancing in the rear view mirror, Hershel appeared to relax. "I suppose you're right. But, I hope we don't have to do anything like that again."

Sally gave him a humoring smile, then both turned their attention to the hills, which they were swiftly approaching.

Up and down they went, around sharp turns, and then the old Dodge would chug along, laboring to climb the next rise.

Hershel would find a place to get off the road and then they would wait until he could put more water in.

That evening, by the time they reached the other side of the hills, they had run out of water.

Hershel tried to coast as much as possible to allow the engine to cool, however, towards the bottom of the last hill, it was obvious the car was overheating.

As the sun set, Hershel turned to Sally, "we'll coast as far as we can. Maybe we can get to somewhere."

The car rolled along until Sally spotted something in the distance, "there's something!"

Hershel studied the small structure, "alright, we'll try to make it. Maybe we can get some water there."

By starting the car, putting it in gear in order to pick up some speed, and then shutting it back off and coasting again, they finally rolled into the driveway of a novelty shop, just as daylight was giving way to night.

Hershel leaned over as Sally looked out her window to examined the building. It was a medium sized adobe store, with several large shop windows in the front. In the corner of one of the windows was a "closed" sign.

The front of the structure had words painted here and there, such as "Indian Blankets," and "Hand Made Jewelry.

"Do you think it's still in business," Sally asked, while holding the pup in her lap.

"Looks like it. I see some stuff in the windows. I suppose we'll have to wait until morning before anyone is around though."

After letting the pup and Mitsy out to use the bathroom, Sally climbed in the back and Hershel laid down on the front seat. Soon they were both sound asleep.

A fresh, cool morning breeze caressed Sally's face as she opened her eyes. Suddenly, she became petrified with fear. A Native American man was standing beside the driver's side window, peering in at her and Hershel. He was in his mid forties, had long black hair that was tied back and distinctive features of what Sally had grown up to know as "Indian."

As her mind and eyes cleared from sleep, she reached over and bumped the front seat to stir Hershel awake.

"Hey, come on, I'm trying to sleep." Hershel mumbled.

"Hershel!" Sally said in a hushed voice, which mattered little as the man could hear her, regardless.

With this prompting from Sally, Hershel opened his eyes, he immediately sat up, almost bumping his head on the roof of the sedan.

"Ohh, uhm, hello, how are you, Sir?"

"I'm very well, how are you?" The man replied with a distinctive accent.

"We're, well, I guess, we're alright. But, our car is not doing very well."

The man stepped back and looked the old car over.

"I hope it's doing better than it looks. Normally, I like having cars in my parking lot, it helps business. But, I think this one may do the opposite."

Hershel and Sally chuckled a little, seeming to still not be fully awake. The man continued.

"Will it run enough to move it around back? We can see about it there."

"Yeah I think so, it shouldn't overheat by moving it that far." Hershel then sat up and started the car. Soon he had it pulled around back and he and Sally got out.

The man studied the two curiously as they stood in their tattered clothes, looking about their surroundings.

Behind the adobe store was a large teepee, with a small circle of rocks in front; obviously used for campfires. At the back of the building, Hershel noticed a late 1940s Chevrolet pick-up parked under what appeared to be a homemade carport. The truck was clean and seemed to be well cared for.

Hershel then turned to the man, who continued to examined them.

"Oh, I'm sorry. My name is Hershel and this is Sally." He then held out his hand and Sally nodded to the man.

"My name is White Feather." He said as he shook Hershel's hand.

"White Feather, that's a real nice name."

"Only if you're Indian," White Feather replied, still expressing some puzzlement with the two visitors.

Sally pointed to the teepee, "do you live there?"

White Feather looked at her and then the teepee.

"No, it's too difficult to run plumbing in there. I have living quarters at the back of the store. But, I do sleep there sometimes."

After a few seconds of silence White Feather asked, "Would you two like a cup of coffee?"

This brought an immediate smile to Sally's face.

"Oh, that would be wonderful, if it's not too much trouble." She replied quickly.

Once inside, they sat at a small table as White Feather prepared some coffee. Soon they were sipping the hot beverage.

"So, what is the problem with your... automobile?"

"The water pump is going out, or, may have already gone out. We ran out of water coming over the hills back there." Hershel then took another drink of his coffee.

"Hmm, I don't sell water pumps here. Only hand crafted items. But they are of a high quality and are genuine Indian made. No fakes."

Sally and Hershel examined White Feather for a few seconds.

"How far is it to the next town or city?" Hershel finally asked.

"Well, there's Oatman, which is around ten miles west of here. But there's not much there. Bullhead city is around sixty five miles from here. It's more like a large town than a city. And, there's the Indian reservation, that's about seventy miles."

"Can we fill our water jugs here?" Hershel asked.

"Yes, you can do that." White Feather replied.

"We might be able to make it to Bullhead city, as long as the water pump hasn't gone out. Is there a salvage yard there?"

"I believe there is a small one. May I ask where you are going to?"

"Los Angeles," Hershel replied.

"Well, Bullhead city is to the Northwest of here. It would be far off your path to Los Angeles."

Hershel and Sally both expressed surprise.

"It's not on highway sixty-six?" Sally asked.

"No, not at all. Beyond the tiny town of Oatman, the next town on sixty-six is Needles California. You must cross the Colorado river. It's around one hundred and fifty miles, with only a few service stations along the way."

Hershel and Sally looked at each other. Hershel turned back to his cup of coffee, which he held on the table with both hands.

Just as Hershel was about to reply, a bell was heard in the store.

"Excuse me, I have a customer. Help yourself to the coffee." White Feather stood and went through a curtain and into the store.

Sally took the coffee pot and poured her another cup, welcoming the rich aroma that flowed from the dark liquid.

"So, what's the plan?" She asked as she poured a bit of sugar and began stirring the coffee.

"I suppose it depends on whether the water pump is shot or not. If it's still working, we can try to go on. We'll just have to stop and fill it with water as before."

Sally examined Hershel briefly.

"And if the water pump is shot?"

Hershel thought for a few seconds; expelled a long breath of air and then replied.. "I don't know. We can't drive the car with it overheating."

Sally frowned, but then looked back at her coffee.

White Feather returned after a few more minutes.

"Are you ready for some breakfast?"

The two visitors looked at him with surprise.

"Well, we don't expect you to feed us, White Feather. You've already done a lot. The coffee and filling our water jugs will be enough."

White Feather walked into the small kitchen area after Hershel said this. He pulled a skillet from a hook and sat it on the stove.

"I don't mind. It's not often I get visitors. Plus you should try my cooking before becoming too grateful."

Sally laughed a bit and Hershel smiled.

"Would you mind if I helped, White Feather?" Sally asked.

"That would be very good. I was hoping you might."

Sally stood up and helped prepare the food. Soon they were eating breakfast at the small table.

Later, Hershel filled the radiator of the old Dodge. He started it and watched. Within a short time, the car was overheating and he had to shut it down.

As steam sprayed from the relief valve on the radiator cap, he and Sally watched with dismay.

"Hmm, I believe that means your water pump is no longer functioning." White Feather said as he approached the two.

"I believe you're right. I was sure hoping for something better." Hershel replied, while waving some of the steam away from his face.

Sally reached down and picked up the puppy, which had been walking around her feet in an effort to gain attention. Hershel backed up some and turned to White Feather.

"I hate to ask you, but, do you go to town very often?"

"No, I never go to town. I do go to the reservation in order to get more product for the store, as well as supplies."

"Does the reservation have a salvage yard?" Hershel asked.

"There is what we call a 'junk' yard. The owner has many broken down cars and such. As well as appliances and other items that he will sell parts off of. I suspect he may have what you need."

"Will you be going there any time soon?" Sally asked as the puppy wriggled about in her hands.

A dusty breeze moved through as White Feather considered this.

"I only go when I need product for the store. So, I must sell a lot of product before there is a need to go." He looked at the two and they expressed disappointment.

"Perhaps there is a way though."

When he said this, Sally and Hershel perked back up.

"If you can help me attract more customers, then I can sell my stock faster, which means I will need to go to the reservation sooner."

"That would be great! But, what can we do to get more customers?" Hershel asked.

White Feather looked the two over, as if sizing them up.

"Oh, I have an idea. Come with me."

A short time later, Sally stepped outside from White Feather's living quarters behind the store. She was dressed as an Indian squaw. She looked down at the costume with apparent doubt.

White Feather leaned against his pick-up under the shade. He chuckled a bit as he examined Sally.

A few seconds after this, Hershel stepped out from the teepee. He was dressed as an Indian brave.

Sally looked at him and he at her. White Feather now laughed a bit as he noticed Hershel.

"I don't know about this, do we really look like Indians?" Sally asked.

White Feather stepped from the shade as Sally and Hershel moved closer.

"No, not at all." The native man replied.

"So, what makes you think this will work?" Her face twisted slightly as she questioned him.

"Because, white people don't know what real Indians look like."

"What makes you say that?"

He turned his attention from her costume and looked at her. Then replied.

"You just asked me if you looked like a real Indian."

Sally's face fell a bit, "Oh, yeah."

White Feather asked Hershel to help him move some rocks around to the front of the store. He then placed them in a small circle as Hershel and Sally brought some wood from a stack around back.

A small fire was built, just large enough to "make some smoke," as White Feather put it. he then went into the store and returned with two small hand instruments that made a raspy sound when shook. Also in his other hand was a small hand held drum.

White Feather gave the instruments to Hershel and Sally. He instructed them a bit on producing a rhythm. Then made some humming and moaning sounds that he felt the white people would certainly mistake as Indian songs.

As he was finishing up the instructions, a large station wagon slowed and stopped; then it pulled into the store parking lot.

"Very good, we've already got customers and you haven't stared dancing yet!" White Feather said with a smile, as a large family got out of the car and walked towards the three.

Sally glanced at Hershel and he looked at her. He then began to tap his drum and with this Sally began shaking the hand held noise makers. They both started to dance around the small fire.

White Feather smiled again as the family began taking pictures and talking about the "Indian dancers."

Thus began Sally and Hershel's Indian dancing stint. They were an immediate hit and on occasions the parking lot was completely filled with cars.

White Feather fed the two, along with some scraps for Mitsy and the pup. Hershel slept on a cot in the teepee and Sally slept in the back seat of the Dodge.

After a very busy week, the three ate their supper out back, in front of the teepee. A small fire was burning as they relaxed after the meal. Sally had the puppy in her arms and Mitsy on her lap, as had become the norm. The night gently took over and darkness enveloped the three, other than the light of the campfire.

Sally leaned back and began looking at the stars.

"They're so beautiful. It's almost like you could reach out and touch them."

White Feather looked up into the sky. "I touch them all the time. It's not a difficult thing to do, if you know how."

Hershel and Sally both turned to him and starred. Silence prevailed, other than the crackling of the fire, then in the distance, a coyote howled.

"What are you talking about?" Sally asked.

White Feather turned his attention to the two, seeming just now to notice they were watching him.

"There's a cactus that has a substance in it. This substance allows one to touch the stars and see the future. Indians have been using it since ancient times."

Still, Hershel and Sally starred at White Feather, seeming to be completely in disbelief.

The lone coyote again howled in the distance. The fire crackled and the smell of Mesquite wood floated fragrantly about.

Finally, White Feather looked a the two and said, "would you like to touch the stars?"

Sally seemed reluctant to answer. But Hershel wasted no time.

"Oh yeah, absolutely!"

She glanced over at Hershel; he was smiling brightly, as a child might with the prospect of getting a chocolate bar.

White Feather went into his living quarters and soon returned with a small wooden box, a pitcher of water and three glasses.

Hershel threw a piece of wood on the fire and then moved over beside White Feather.

Sally huffed a bit, under her breath, but soon moved over closer to them as well.

"So, what is this... substance?" Hershel asked as White Feather took a knife and cut pieces of dried cactus, that had been cleaned of needles, into smaller sections.

"The white man calls it 'peyote,' and it would matter little to you what my tribe calls it. The Indians have long used it in ceremonies and for matters of the spirit world. It is not a common thing for an Indian to offer such a thing to the white man."

Sally immediately asked, "so why are you offering it to us?"

White Feather glanced up to her, "because I foresaw you coming here some time back. It was while I was using the peyote. In my vision, I offered the two of you an opportunity to touch the stars. It was the future, and now it is the present and I fulfill that vision."

Sally and Hershel again studied the man with wonder.

"So, you saw us before we came here?" Sally asked.

"Well, I didn't know it was you, because I didn't know you then. But, as time has passed, I've realized it was you."

White Feather then handed each one five slim slices of the cactus. He then poured a glass of water for the three of them.

"Like this," he said, then swallowed a slice and drank some water.

Sally's face winced a bit. Then it turned to shock as Hershel immediately followed White Feather's instructions.

As White Feather and Hershel were downing their second piece, Sally asked, "is this going to make me sick?"

"I can't say for certain, but it doesn't make me sick." White Feather replied.

Hershel had by now downed his last piece.

"Come on, Sally, it's just cactus."

She looked at the two; her face was slightly twisted. Then she slowly raised the piece of peyote to her mouth and swallowed it; immediately followed with water. She repeated this process until all five were gone.

They sat watching the fire and Sally took turns petting Mitsy and the puppy. The coyote again howled in the distance and was met this time by several other coyote howls from a different area.

White Feather sat with an odd smile on his face. The fire crackled and embers danced into the air.

"I don't think that cactus stuff works on white people," Sally finally said.

White Feather laughed a bit, under his breath. Then Sally noticed his face seeming to melt. She shook her head and looked at Hershel. He had a smile on his face and it also seemed to be dropping, as if slowly melting.

She looked down at the puppy, which was trying to crawl up to her face. It suddenly became the most adorable thing she had ever seen. she picked it up and a bright smile erupted onto her face.

"Awww, you're soooo cute!" She said, while holding it in front of her.

Looking over to Hershel and White Feather, she realized they were starring bright eyed at the fire. Both, then began to laugh.

Sally then noticed how bright and beautiful the flames were. All three sat and watched the campfire for some time.

Later Hershel and Sally were dancing, Indian style, around the fire. They stopped and laughed again.

Sally still held the puppy. She lifted it up for Hershel to see and with a beaming smile said, "I'm going to name it, 'Spot!'"

Hershel laughed and appeared to have a little trouble standing.

"But it doesn't have any spots!" He exclaimed with an equally brilliant smile.

"I know! That's just it!" She laughed and Hershel broke out in more laughter as well.

Some time later, White Feather watched the two as they held their hands up to the night sky.

"You really can touch them," Sally said as she sat directly beside Hershel.

"They're amazing," Hershel replied.

More dancing and laughing occurred as the night moved closer to morning. The fire began to die down and the small group finally fell asleep, exhausted from the eventful evening.

As the sun broke across the horizon, Sally was stirred from sleep by the pup licking her face. Raising up some, she realized her head was laying on Hershel's chest.

"Ahhggggg, what is going on?" She stood up and Hershel abruptly woke with her loud question.

"What did you do! Tell me right now... you... snake!!"

Hershel sat up on his elbows, his eyes were still blinking as he tried to wake up.

"What are you talking about?" He asked.

"You know what I'm talking about! What did you do?" She stomped around rubbing her messy hair.

"I don't know what you're talking about, Sally"

"Oh yeah? Then why was we... like, you know...that?" She waved her hands, indicating the situation she awoke to.

Hershel strained to understand, seeming still not awake.

"Like what?" He finally asked.

"You know what! I knew I shouldn't have trusted you. I knew it.... Men, they're all alike!"

White Feather had sat up on one elbow and was now laughing in a subdued manner.

"And you!" She pointed at White Feather. "You said we would see the future!"

White Feather laughed even more when she said this, but then replied, "I didn't say when you would see it."

"Ahggg," she turned and started to storm off. Then she stopped and went back to Hershel, reached down and picked the puppy up.

"Come on, Spot." Holding Spot in her arm, she pointed at White Feather and then Hershel, "I don't want any more of that... cactus!"

Sally then marched off towards the old Dodge.

Hershel and White Feather watched her until she had climbed into the back seat of the car.

"She's a little bit crazy, isn't she?" White Feather asked, still leaning on one elbow.

Hershel considered this as Mitsy climbed up to his chest. He picked her up and began petting the kitten.

"The way I see it, she's more than just a little bit." He finally replied.

White Feather laid back down. The fire smoldered and a breeze moved the smoke around the small campsite.

"I've found that the crazy ones are the best choice, if a man should decide he wants a woman. They make life interesting."

Hershel glanced over to White Feather, who gazed up into the morning sky.

Mitsy purred and snuggled up to Hershel's neck.

"Well, she's certainly done that," he finally said.

The old Indian turned and looking at Hershel, smiled.

Sally calmed down some as morning moved to afternoon. The following day was Monday. Though she still spoke very little to the two men, she did put her costume on and performed out front with Hershel.

Once again, the tourists on their way to and from California stopped and shopped at the store.

"We've done well. In fact, I'll need to close the store and go to the reservation this Friday."

The three sat at the small table drinking coffee. Sally and Hershel perked up when they heard this.

"Great, but, well, do you have any tools?" Hershel asked.

"I have a few. I think enough to take a water pump off and install another one."

Hershel immediately relaxed a bit.

"That's good. I was wondering how I would replace one without tools."

Early Friday morning, the three loaded into the front of White Feather's pick-up and were soon headed west.

After a lengthy drive, they arrived at the reservation. White Feather shopped for his crafts and Hershel helped load and secure them in the back of the pick up.

Then, they went to a large junk yard that had old cars, appliances and various types construction equipment. Hershel found several vehicles with the type of water pump he needed and after careful consideration purchased and removed the pump he felt was the best option.

By the time they returned to the store, the sun was settling on the horizon.

The following day, Sally and Hershel volunteered to do their performance; realizing White Feather had lost revenue from being closed on Friday.

As White Feather restocked and tended the store, Hershel and Sally did their Indian dance routine one more day.

When Sunday morning arrived, Hershel installed the water pump and checked to be sure it was working. Then they spent the reminder of the day packing and preparing to leave the following morning.

As the sun broke over the horizon on Monday morning, Hershel, Sally and White Feather sat at the small table. They had finished their breakfast and were now drinking another cup of coffee.

"We really want to thank you for everything," Hershel said.

"Yeah, White Feather, you've been such a great help to us." Sally added.

White Feather smiled subtly. "We've helped each other. That is the way it should be. It is what the Great Spirit wishes for all of mankind."

Shortly after this they said their good-byes. Hershel and Sally climbed into the old sedan and were soon heading west.

Chapter Eleven: *A La Natural*

Hershel glanced over to Sally. The warm breeze flowed through the car and constantly blew her hair about. She alternated between petting Spot and Mitsy, then attempted to brush the hair from her eyes.

Sally noticed Hershel looking at her. She smiled slightly, seeming glad to be back on the road.

After stopping at the tiny town of Oatman for gas, they continued on.

Before nightfall they were both very excited to cross the Colorado river and arrive in California. They passed through Needles and then stopped to sleep.

The next morning, Sally crawled out from the back of the car. Hershel had a California map, which White Feather had given him, spread out over the hood.

Sally came up beside him and studied the map.

"Well, are we going to make it?" She asked.

"It's going to be close. This old Dodge uses a lot of gas, and burns oil like crazy. With the money we've got, it's going to be very close."

Hershel pointed to the map. "We're around here. Over here is Los Angeles and Hollywood.

After looking over the map a few seconds, Sally replied, "that doesn't look so bad."

"It's a couple hundred miles, at least." Hershel said.

"Really? it doesn't look that far."

Hershel smiled, "not on a map. But from what little I know of them, we've still got a ways to go."

He then began to fold the map up and they were soon back on the road.

By noon, Hershel knew the old sedan was having trouble. It began to smoke more and the engine was making a rattling sound.

He stopped and after checking the oil, found it was very low. He put more oil in and they continued.

By that evening, the car was making a terrible sound. It had almost no power and was smoking very badly.

Suddenly, a loud bang was heard; Sally screamed a bit with shock and the car shuddered as the engine went dead.

Hershel shifted the car into neutral and coasted. He turned onto a dirt road and around a hundred feet from the highway, the car rolled to a stop.

"What now?" Sally asked.

"I don't know, but it sounded very bad."

Hershel climbed out and was soon shining the flashlight around the engine.

"Well?" Sally came up beside him, holding Mitsy.

"It threw a rod, straight through the engine block."

Sally leaned over to look in the area that Hershel was pointing the flashlight.

"Is that bad?" She asked.

Hershel glanced at her. "It's about as bad as it can get."

"Can you fix it?"

Hershel straightened up and took a deep breath, then expelled it.

"No, I don't know a whole lot about rebuilding Dodge engines. And, I don't have the tools to do it, even if I did know enough to try... The only reason I know what's wrong is one of the cars I replaced the engine in for Skinny had the same issue. Skinny said the best option is to swap the motor out with another one."

Sally moaned in frustration. "Wonderful, so we're afoot again."

"It seems so."

"Maybe we could sell the car to somebody."

Hershel considered this. "I don't think so. Skinny didn't give us a title and the license plate is seven years out of date. Actually, I think we can sleep in it tonight, but we should probably try to gain some distance from it first thing in the morning."

"Why?" She asked.

"Well, if a Highway Patrolman finds us with the car, he may try to charge us to have it towed."

Sally's face expressed fright.

"Yeah, I see what you mean. We'll leave first thing in the morning then."

As the sun crept over the horizon the following morning, Hershel and Sally set out on foot again.

Several miles from the abandon Dodge, they caught a ride, which carried them to Amboy. There they shared a hamburger and some coffee.

They left Amboy and caught another ride that took them ten miles west of Ludlow.

It was late afternoon as they walked along the highway and began to desperately search for some place to stay the night. As the evening settled in, cars seldom passed and traffic slowed.

"There's nothing! We're in the middle of nowhere, Hershel!"

He glanced back and saw that Sally was falling behind. She was carrying Spot and appeared exhausted. They had been walking for several hours and the daylight was almost gone.

"Well find something. Or maybe we'll get a ride." He replied.

"A ride from who? There's no one on the rode. They're in motels or campgrounds already."

Hershel grimaced. She was right, and as far as he could see there was nothing; not a building in sight. On both sides there was only sand and sagebrush. He shuddered when thinking of how many rattlesnakes must be around. Not to mention scorpions, spiders and who knew what else.

He continued in the dimming light and arid heat.

"Hershel, slow down!"

"We can't, Sally. We've got to find some place to stay." He continued at the same pace, determined to get somewhere, anywhere that was safe.

As darkness came over the entire area, Hershel pulled the flashlight out. He knew the batteries wouldn't last long.

Sally began to whine, "My feet are hurting, can we stop?"

Hershel came back to her. "Give me your bag."

She shifted Spot to her other hand and slid the blouse bag from her shoulder. Hershel took it and turned back to the highway and started walking again.

As the night became complete, Hershel turned the flashlight on for a few minutes and then turned it off for a few minutes. He felt the road under his feet more than he could see it when the flashlight was off.

Behind him, he could hear Sally trudging along. Other than their feet moving on the road, there were few noises of any kind.

The two struggled along in this manner for several hours. Then Hershel heard Sally stop. He turned the flashlight to her and as soon as it shined on her, she knelt down and then sat on the side of the highway.

"I can't go any farther. I can't, I'm too tired. Let's just stay here."

Spot crawled up to her face and began licking her chin. Hershel walked back towards her.

"We can't stay here, Sally. There's... who knows what on the side of the road; snakes, spiders... who knows. We've got to keep moving. We'll find something."

"I don't care. I can't go any farther. I can't, Hershel."

He examined her face, it expressed defeat. She was obviously exhausted. He considered what to do. After a few more seconds, he knew they must start moving again, the flashlight was quickly growing weak.

"Do you need a spanking, Sally?"

Her expression changed immediately. She looked up at him. Her eyes held surprise and a little fear.

"Maybe... who's going to give it to me?"

Hershel struggled to repress a smile, as she stared at him.

"I might, if you don't get up. We'll find some place, but we've got to keep moving. It's not safe here."

"Hershel..." She whined, her eyes expressing bewilderment.

"Come on." He walked over and reaching down took Spot. Then he took her hand and helped her up.

Sally took hold of the back of Hershel's tattered shirt. He then lead her along the desolate highway.

Around what Hershel though to be midnight. He caught a glimpse of something from the corner of his eye.

The flashlight was barely glowing now, but there was something off to the side of the road.

He stopped and shined the dim light towards the dark shape.

There, off the side of the road was a large bulldozer.

"Come on, Sally" He said, though she seemed to be barely awake.

Carefully, Hershel moved them through the brush and sand. Looking around, he could barely make out other pieces of construction equipment.

Moving past a large crane, he spotted prefabricated, concrete drain sections. They were square and around four feet by six feet.

Helping Sally along, he moved them to the drainage sections. Then he helped her into one that was stacked on others. This kept her around four feet off the ground. She lay down, he gave her Spot, then moved to the drainage section next to hers.

"Hey, where did you go?" Sally mumbled.

He moved back over and glanced in.

"I'm right over here, right next to you."

"I don't like that. I don't know where we are. Don't leave me."

Hershel examined the situation as the flashlight was almost completely dead.

"Sally, there's not much room here."

"I don't care," She mumbled again. then he heard her say, "I've still got my knife. You better be good."

He smiled, "I'm sure you do, Sally. Don't worry."

He crawled in beside her and lay down. Using their bags as pillows, both were soon fast asleep.

The next morning, Hershel woke to the sound of an engine starting. He nudged Sally.

"Hey, we better get out of here."

As she tried to wake up, he slipped out of the drainage section and looked around. There was a pick-up beside a road grader. It looked to be the site foreman, starting the equipment up.

Sally climbed out holding Spot and the two slipped away from the site, keeping low in order to not be seen by the construction foreman.

Once they made it to the highway, they stood straight and walked by the area casually. As they did so, another pick-up pulled up beside the crane.

About a half mile west of the construction equipment, they came to a site being prepared for the drainage sections. There was no water to be seen as they walked along a short detour around the assembling workers and equipment.

"Why would they put those things here if there's no water?" Sally asked.

"I guess when it does rain, it washes down this area quickly, for a short time. Like a flash flood, maybe."

Sally nodded as she examined the site.

Eventually they caught a ride, and that afternoon were dropped off in Barstow.

Standing in front of a cafe, Sally spoke solemnly, "we better not go in, we both smell real bad. Nether one of us has had a bath in days."

Hershel lifted his arm and sniffed. He grimaced and lowered it quickly.

"There's a service station down the road, maybe we can get cleaned up."

She glanced at him.

"It wouldn't matter, we don't have anything clean to wear."

They both turned and again looked wishfully at the cafe.

Suddenly, Sally perked up, "Hey, maybe we do have something clean, or at least cleaner."

She took the wicker case from Hershel. After opening it and pulling out some odds and ends, she pulled the clothes Libby had given them up from the very bottom.

160

Hershel looked at the odd attire as she lifted a mans shirt up to him.

"Well, I suppose anything would be an improvement right now." He said.

She handed the shirt to him and then pulled an obviously outdated dress out.

"Yeah, well, I figure we'll get noticed wearing this stuff, but it'll be better than getting noticed for smelling bad."

Hershel chuckled about this and they walked to the service station to clean up.

Later they sat in the cafe, finishing a hamburger and fries, split between them, and drinking coffee.

Sally examined Hershel's odd clothing, which was rather comical. The pants came up above his waist and were obviously something from the nineteen twenties. She suggested he leave the shirt un-tucked after first seeing this, but he said that looked even worse since the shirt had been made to be tucked into the pants. Not doing this made it look like he was wearing a blouse or short dress.

Sally's donated clothes were not much better. The dress was tight on her chest, and she often squirmed with discomfort and an effort to readjust the top part of the dress. Also, it had frilly rows of tiny tassels dangling; causing a "vibrating" effect every time she moved.

The waitress brought the ticket and laid it on the table. She smiled and said, "I like your dress."

Sally glanced up to her. "Thanks... we're uhm, headed to a costume party."

The waitress became excited, "I thought it was something like that. Lucy and I was just talking about it, I said you two may be dressed up for some sort of costume get-together."

Sally gave the woman a tight lipped smile and nodded.

Once the waitress had left, Sally looked at the ticket and seemed to be calculating in her mind. After a few seconds and a drink of coffee she looked at Hershel.

"We could get a bus to Los Angeles from here, but that would take most of our money. We have around twenty-three dollars and some change. If we keep going like we are now and split that in Los Angeles, it will give each of us about eleven dollars to get by on until we can get some work."

When Sally said this, Hershel's eyes dropped and he looked into his coffee cup.

Sally continued.

"That's not much, but it's better than nothing. As bad as I hate to say it. I think we need to hitchhike into Los Angeles and save every dime we can for when we get there."

She looked at Hershel, waiting for his response. He continued to look at his coffee.

"What do you think?" She asked.

"Yeah, that seems to be the best thing. It's not that much farther."

Sally nodded, "We should probably find a place here to stay tonight. Maybe the bus station. Then leave early in the morning."

Hershel looked at her and answered in a subdued voice, "Yeah, that would be best."

That night they slept on a bench outside the bus station.

The following morning they ate toast and drank some coffee at the cafe, then started walking out of town.

By noon, they had made it to Victorville, where they were let off.

Once again, they walked to the outskirts of town, with hopes of making it to San Bernardino by nightfall.

A short ways outside of Victorville, they passed by a small novelty shop and beside that was an artist's studio. Outside the studio, leaning against the walls of the entrance, were numerous landscape and animal paintings, such as horses and dogs.

Sally examined the artist's work as they walked past. Then she grabbed Hershel's arm and they stopped.

"What?" he asked and looked at what she was pointing to.

In the window was a sign that read, "Models Wanted."

"Let's check it out," she said and they walked into the open doorway.

At the rear of the studio sat a man in his thirties, behind a small counter that had an old cash register sitting on it. He was reading a large book, but glanced up at the two as they came closer.

"We were wondering about the modeling job." Sally asked.

The man closed the book, but held the place with his thumb. He sat up and looked them both over.

"I don't need any male models." He then examined Sally closely, from head to toe.

"You'll work though." He paused and looked at her head. "We'll need to do something with that hair, but that shouldn't be much trouble."

Sally glanced at Hershel and smiled excitedly.

"That's great! So, how long are we talking about?"

"A couple hours should be sufficient." The man replied, seeming almost bored with the discussion.

Again Sally looked at Hershel, who also had a slight smile.

"That's perfect!" She stepped closer to the counter.

"So, how much pay are we talking about?"

"Forty dollars," the man replied.

"Forty dollars? Oh, well that is great!"

"Yes, well if your ready, we can get started, I'll need to close the studio while we're working."

Sally nodded, "alright, wonderful, what do I need to do?"

The man stood up and pointed to a door behind the counter.

"The studio is back there, you can go back and get undressed. I'll be back after I get everything inside."

The smile on Sally's face dropped a bit.

"Uhm, is there a costume back there for me to wear?"

The man had walked around the counter and was heading towards the front, but he stopped and looked at Sally.

"No, I'll be painting you in your birthday suit."

Sally's nose crinkled a little after hearing this. Hershel began to look around at the paintings inside. Mixed in with a variety of miscellaneous subjects were many of women, all wearing nothing.

"Uhm, birthday suit?" Sally asked, as if not understanding.

The man expressed a slight smile, "yes, you know, *'a la natural'*," he said, adding a slight French accent.

Sally raised her finger, "give us just a minute."

The man nodded and walked back around the counter, picking his book back up.

Sally pulled Hershel towards the front of the store.

"Let's just go." Hershel said.

"No, let me think about this." She replied in a hushed voice.

"What's to think about, Sally?"

Her face was twisted in thought. She put the tip of her thumb in her mouth and briefly chewed on the nail.

"Forty dollars is a lot of money right now. We're in a desperate situation Hershel."

Hershel stared at her for several seconds as she stared across the room in thought.

"We're not that desperate, Sally. I can't believe you're even considering it."

She looked at him, her face expressed concern and fear both.

"Well, we're almost broke. We need money. It's just two hours... I mean, maybe it wouldn't be so bad."

Hershel became very serious.

"Sally, when you get to Hollywood, people are going to ask you to do things; things you don't want to do. They'll offer you money, probably a lot of money, to do things you really don't want to do. If you start doing those things now, where will it stop?"

She looked at him. She considered this. Again she bit her thumbnail.

"Yeah, I know. But, well, maybe just this once. I mean, who's going to know?"

Now he looked her straight in the eyes.

"You'll know, Sally."

Her eyes dropped and she again starred across the room while considering his words. A few seconds later she walked to the front of the store.

"I'm sorry, you'll need to get another model."

The man glanced up from the book, "sure." He then went right back to his reading.

A few minutes later they were again trudging down the side of the dusty highway.

Chapter Twelve: Because it's the Truth

They arrived at San Bernardino that evening and slept in a park.

The following morning they sat in a restaurant, once again eating toast and drinking coffee. Sally reached under the table, opened the wicker case and gave Mitsy and Spot a small piece of toast, then shut the case lid back.

After their small meal, the two again began hitchhiking.

As the cars went by, the breeze would blow Sally's dress around, causing it to shimmer and appear to vibrate. Hershel smiled and chuckled a bit as he watched her holding a thumb out, trying to catch a ride.

They soon made it to the West side of Pasadena. It was in the afternoon and they began walking out of town. After walking for several miles, they came up over a small ridge and Hershel stopped.

Sally had Spot in one hand and was looking down as she followed him. When Hershel stopped she looked up and noticed what he was starring at. Immediately she let out a shout of joy.

They stood in front of a sign that read "Welcome to Los Angeles."

He turned to her and she turned to him. Without much thought, she gave him a hug. As they embraced, she looked up to him with a smile. Hershel then leaned down and kissed her. For a brief instant she kissed him back.

Then, she pulled away from him and hit him on the chest with her free hand.

"What did you do that for?" She shouted.

"Because, I love you Sally."

"Don't say that! Stop it, Hershel! Why did you say that?"

"Because it's the truth. I love you and I want to marry you. Will you marry me, Sally?"

Sally moved around as if in a trap of some type. She put her hand up to her head as she seemed to be on the verge of exploding. She then stopped and starred at him.

"Hershel, we're standing on the side of the road! We're... we're wearing donated clothes that are older than we are. We don't have a thing... except a dog and a cat.. that we can barely feed. And you're talking about love and marriage? We've got nothing, Hershel... nothing!"

Hershel stepped closer to her. She stepped back, still holding Spot, and expressing fear.

"That's not the way I see it, Sally. The way I see it, we've got what we had when we started traveling together in Oklahoma. All we really had then was each other. But that's been enough to get us halfway across the country."

Sally's expression of fear began to fall from her face. Hershel took another step towards her and this time she didn't step back.

"But, after we pass that sign, there's a chance I could lose you. And that scares me, Sally. That scares me more than anything we've faced or anything we might face on the other side of that sign.

"The way I see it, as long as we're together, we can do anything we set our minds to and we'll always be alright. But I'm not sure about that if we lose each other. If I don't have you with me, I'm not sure that I'll be alright."

Sally stared at him. He then noticed a single tear erupt from her eye and roll down her check. Still she made no move.

A car flew past them and caused her dress to shimmer from the breeze. Spot wiggled in her hand.

Sally raised her free hand and stepped towards him. He stiffened up a bit, ready for her to hit him again.

She did hit him very lightly on the chest, but then embraced him.

He looked down at her and she raised her face to him. Tears were rolling down her checks now.

Leaning down, he kissed her again, and she kissed him back.

After the passionate kiss, he asked, "does that mean what I think it means?"

She laughed a little, with tears still in her eyes.

"Yes, it means yes, I'll marry you."

She continued to hold onto him, "you're crazy though, you know that don't you?"

Hershel smiled, "I'm thinking that will be a plus."

Then, hand in hand, they crossed into Los Angeles.

Later that evening, they sat at an outside table of a burger drive-in. Spot and Mitsy played at their feet and Hershel dropped two small pieces of his hamburger on the ground for them.

Sally glanced at him, her eyes sparkled.

"So, what's the plan?" She asked and then finished up the last bite of her burger.

Hershel considered this briefly.

"Well, I think we need to get grandmother settled as soon as possible. Then, we should get married. After that, we'll find a place to live. We may need to stay in a shelter for a while. But I'll get a job as a mechanic. You can start looking for acting jobs as soon as we can get you some nice clothes."

She rubbed his arm lovingly.

"Hmm, a honeymoon in a shelter?"

"I suspect it'll be better than in a tank." He then winked at her.

She laughed.

"Yeah, you're probably right about that. But, we've got around twenty dollars. It'll take half of that to get a marriage license and then have a simple ceremony somewhere. Shouldn't we wait on that?"

"Hmm," he rubbed his chin in thought, then reached down into his sock and pulled out two five dollar bills that were folded up.

"No, I really don't want to wait." He said, holding them up.

"Where did you get that? You sly dog... You've been holding out on me! How long have you had that?"

"Oh, I put it back when we worked with Tex. The 'sock money' advice from my brother has actually worked out fairly well."

She smiled and pushed his arm lovingly.

"Well, I don't want to touch it! But, if you really want to spend it on a wedding, I'm game."

They slept at a bus station that night. The following morning they made their way to the cemetery that Hershel had been directed to take his grandmother's ashes to.

After several bus rides and a lengthy walk, they arrived at the gate of an extravagant, private cemetery. There was a guard outside and he stopped the two at the entry way.

"Can I help you?" the burly man asked.

"I'm Hershel Lawson. I'm bringing my grandmother's ashes to be housed here. I was told to speak with the director."

The guard looked at the two suspiciously.

"And what was your grandmother's name?"

"Ethel Lawson." Hershel replied.

"Just a moment," The man stepped into the gatehouse and picked up a phone. Soon he was talking to someone and a few minutes later stepped back out.

"You can go in. Follow the road to the main building, there you should ask for Mr. Nelson. He'll lead you to where your grandmother is to be placed."

The two moved towards a sizable and opulent structure at the end of the drive.

There were large marble columns in front as they arrived at the lavish, white building. Stepping in through ornate doors, they moved across polished marble floors to the front desk.

"May I help you?" Asked a very beautiful and well dressed secretary at the front desk.

"We're here to see Mr. Nelson."

As Hershel said this, a man came from a back room. He was in his forties, had dark hair and was also dressed very well.

"Mr Nelson, these people are here to see you."

The man came closer.

"You are, Hershel Lawson?"

"Yes Sir."

Mr. Nelson examined the battered clothes they wore and the shoddy baggage in their arms. His eyes squinted slightly with obvious disdain.

"I'll need to see some identification, if you don't mind."

"Oh, yeah, sure." Hershel then took out his wallet and confirmed who he was.

"Follow me please," Mr. Nelson then began walking to the rear of the building.

Hershel and Sally followed him out a back door that opened to a beautiful cemetery. There were hundreds of marvelous mausoleums, all made from various colors of marble.

They continued along a concrete pathway, passing several uniformed caretakers along the way.

"After you've placed your grandmother, I'll need you to sign some papers. You can also verify all transactions, I have all the receipts on file." Mr. Nelson said, while glancing back.

Sally marveled at flower bushes and the air was sweetly scented from the many exotic plants.

"Honestly, I had begun to wonder about the situation, Mr. Lawson. It's been some time since I received word of your grandmother's passing."

Mr. Nelson glanced back again as he continued to lead the way.

"Yes, I uhm, ran into some difficulties along the way."

"I see." Mr. Nelson then stopped in front of a large and exquisite, marble mausoleum.

Hershel immediately noticed a small, brass, letter slot at the side of the door. Sally examined the front and then stared at the small letter slot with curiosity.

"Here you are Mr. Lawson. You'll find a letter addressed to you in here, as your grandmother requested." Mr. Nelson then pulled an envelope from an inside jacket pocket.

"Once again, after checking that everything is to your satisfaction, please be sure to stop by and sign the paperwork before you leave."

Mr. Nelson handed the envelope to Hershel, then started walking away.

Hershel glanced at the envelope.

"You think she was planning to get mail?" Sally asked, pushing open the brass door on the letter slot with her finger.

Hershel shrugged his shoulders, then took hold of the handle and tried to open the large ornate door. It was locked.

"Uhm, excuse me! Mr. Nelson!" He shouted as the man was about to round the corner of another mausoleum.

Mr. Nelson stopped and stepped back towards them.

"Yes Mr. Lawson, what is it?"

"The door, it's locked."

Mr Nelson, expressed surprise.

"Of course it is, Mr. Lawson."

Hershel expressed confusion. "Well, do you have a key?"

"Certainly not."

"You don't? Then who does?" Hershel asked.

"You should have it. It's in the urn. Did your grandmother not tell you anything?"

Hershel expressed a bit of embarrassment. "I guess she didn't get a chance to tell me that."

"Yes, well you should take a look in the envelope, perhaps her letter will explain." Mr. Nelson then turned and walked around the corner.

Hershel handed the envelope to Sally and then sat some of his things down.

"Can you read the letter while I look for the key?"

Sally looked at the letter. "Are you sure?"

He had begun to pull the battered case, which held the urn from a makeshift bag. He looked up to her.

"Sally, after we get this taken care of, we're going to be married. You'll be my wife. Yes, I'm sure, go ahead and read it out loud. I' sure my grandmother would have loved you."

He opened the case as Sally took the letter from the envelope.

The urn had a strip of tape around the lid. Hershel pulled this off as Sally began reading.

"'My dear Hershel. Since you are reading this, it is certain that you've made it to my final resting place, just as I knew you would do.'"

Opening the lid, Hershel found there was another lid inside that protected the ashes and a set of keys rested in the pocket area between the inner lid and outer lid.

Taking the keys out he replaced the outer lid and stood back up. Sally continued.

"'I have known for a long time that you were capable of great things and could make your own way. But, you've devoted much of your life caring for me in my twilight years.'"

Hershel unlocked the door and opened it. They stepped in as Sally continued.

"'I felt you needed to get out some and thought a nice drive to California would help. Also it would be good for you to gain some distance from your older brother, under the circumstances.'"

Inside the mausoleum, there was a large, marble pedestal directly across from the entrance. All over the floor and heaped in front of the letter slot, were hundreds of sealed envelopes.

Sally stopped reading and glanced at the mound of letters on the floor. She then stepped aside as Hershel sat everything on the floor other than the urn. Sally began reading again.

"'Because of your devotion, and the selfless care you have given to your grandmother, I've left you the bulk of my estate, here in the mausoleum. There are stocks, bonds and cash here, which totals a value of around, ONE POINT FIVE MILLION DOLLARS!!, or so my accountant tells me!'" Sally's face lit up and her voice became very excited. She went on as Hershel lifted the urn and placed it on the pedestal.

"I hope during the trip here your horizons have been broadened and boundaries expanded, if only in a small way. But more importantly, I think you should stay in California and not mention the inheritance to your brother. He would possibly contest it, and this would only lead to problems for the both of you.

"'I love you very dearly and I thank you for so many years of sacrifice in caring for me. If you are careful with this money, it should last you a lifetime. It is my thanks to you. Take care, my dear grandson, Love, Me'ma.'"

Sally began to look at all the envelopes on the floor.

Hershel carefully adjusted the urn on the pedestal and then, staring at it, rubbed the side lovingly with his thumb.

Sally quickly opened one of the envelopes from the floor.

"Hershel! There's thousands of dollars, in this envelope alone!" Her voice cracked with excitement.

Hershel's eyes remained fixed on the urn, his thumb rubbing the side softly as a slight smile broke across his face.

"Did you hear me, Hershel? You're rich! Your rich, Hershel!"

He continued to smile, but never turned from the urn. Finally, in a soft voice he replied.

"No Sally... we're rich."

The End

Thank you for reading A Life Naive. We hope you enjoyed it. Please check out all of Oliver Phipps' works online. For your convenience, we've listed a few of them here that you may also be interested in.

Twelve Minutes till Midnight

A man catches a ride on a dusty Louisiana road only to find he's traveling with notorious outlaws Bonnie and Clyde.

The suspense is nonstop as confrontation settles in between a man determined to stand on truth and an outlaw determined to dislocate him from it.

If your life is subject to living a lie rather than holding to the truth, which would you do?

"Twelve Minutes till Midnight will take you on an unforgettable ride."

Ghosts of Company K: Based on a true story

Tag along with young Bud Fisher during his daily adventures in this ghostly tale based on actual events. It's 1971 and Bud and his family move into an old house in Northern Arkansas. Bud soon discovers they live not far from a very interesting cave as well as a historic Civil War battle site. As odd things start to happen, Bud tries to solve the mysteries. But soon the entire family experiences a haunting situation.

If you enjoy ghost tales based on true events then you'll enjoy Ghosts of Company K. This heartwarming story brings the reader into the life and experiences of a young boy growing up in the early 1970s. Seen through innocent and unsuspecting eyes, Ghosts of Company K reveals a haunting tale from the often unseen perspective of a young boy.

Where the Strangers Live

When a passenger plane disappears over the Indian Ocean in autumn 2013, a massive search gets underway.

A deep trolling, unmanned pod picks up faint readings and soon the deep sea submersible Oceana and her three crew members are four miles below the ocean surface in search of the black box from flight N340.

Nothing could have prepared the submersible crew for what they discover and what happens afterwards. Ancient evils and other world creatures challenge the survival of the Oceana's crew. Secrets of the past are revealed, but death hangs in the balance for Sophie, Troy and Eliot in this deep sea Science Fiction thriller.

A Tempest Soul

Seventeen year old Gina Falcone has been alone for much of her life. Her father passed away while she was young. Her un-affectionate mother eventually leaves her to care for herself when she is only thirteen.

Though her epic journey begins by an almost deadly mistake, Gina will find many of her hearts desires in the most unlikely of places. The loss of everything is the catalyst that brings her to an unimagined level of accomplishment in her life.

Yet Gina soon realizes it is the same events that brought her success that may also bring everything crashing down around her. The new life she has built soon beckons for something she left behind. Now the new woman must find a way to dance through a life she could have never dreamed of.

Diver Creed Station

Wars, disease and a massive collapse of civilization have ravaged the human race of a hundred years in the future. Finally in the late twenty-second century, mankind slowly begins to struggle back from the edge of extinction.

When a huge "virtual life" facility is restored from a hibernation type of storage and slowly brought back online, a new hope materializes.

Fragments of humanity begin to move into the remnants of Denver and the Virtua-Gauge facilities, which offer seven days of virtual leisure for seven days work in this new and growing social structure.

Most inhabitants of this new lifestyle begin to hate the real world and work for the seven day period inside the virtual pods. It's the variety of luxury role play inside the virtual zone that supply's the incentive needed to work hard for seven days in the real world.

In this new social structure a man can work for seven days in a food dispersal unit and earn seven days as a twenty-first century software billionaire in the virtual zone. As time goes by and more of the virtual pods are brought back online life appears to be getting better.

Rizette and her husband Oray are young technicians that settle into their still new marriage as the virtual facilities expand and thrive.

Oray has recently attained the level of a Class A Diver and enjoys his job. The Divers are skilled technicians that perform critical repairs to the complex system, from inside the virtual zone.

His title of Diver originates from often working in the secure "lower levels" of the system. These lower level areas are the dividing space between the real world and the world of the virtual zone. When the facility was built, the original designers intentionally placed this buffer zone in the system to avoid threats from non-living virtual personnel.

As Oray becomes more experienced in his elite technical position as a Diver, he is approached by his virtual assistant and forced to make a difficult decision. Oray's decision triggers events that soon pull him and his wife Rizette into a deadly quest for survival.

The stage becomes a massive and complex maze of virtual world sequences as escape or entrapment hang on precious threads of information.

System ghosts from the distant past intermingle with mysterious factions that have thrown Oray and Rizette into a cyberspace trap with little hope for survival.

Ever the Wayward Sky

The Civil War is over. But for Sergeant James Taft, there seems to be no end in sight. He had seldom considered what he would do after the war, because he never believed he would live through it.

James briefly returns to Pennsylvania in an unsuccessful attempt to work as a farmer. He then sets out to find peace and somehow vanquish the ghosts in his soul. What he can't possibly foresee, as he rides west, is the epic story of tragedy, triumph and finding oneself.

"It's unfortunate, but true, that darkness must often be complete before we notice the subtle glimmer of hope." - Doc Jefferies, Ever the Wayward Sky.

Tears of Abandon

Several college friends start planning a two week kayak trip down an Alaskan river in late summer of 1992. Soon there are five young people headed to Alaska for a river expedition.

As the trip unfolds and the group gets farther into the wilderness a strange whispering sound attracts their attention. The wonderful vacation begins to take a turn for the worse when they follow the sounds and find something long lost and quiet unexpected.

Bane of the Innocent

"There's no reason for them to shoot us; we ain't anyone" - Sammy, Bane of the Innocent.

Two young boys become unlikely companions during the fall of Atlanta. Sammy and Ben somehow find themselves, and each other, in the rapidly changing and chaotic environment of the war torn Georgia City.

As the siege ends and the fall begins in late August and early September of 1864 the Confederate troops begin to move out and Union forces cautiously move into the city. Ben and Sammy simply struggle to survive, but in the process they develop a friendship that will prove more important than either one could imagine.

The House on Cooper Lane: Based on a true story

It's 1984 and all Bud Fisher wants to do is find a place to live in Madison Louisiana. With his dog Badger, they come across a beautiful old mansion that was converted into apartments.

Something should have felt odd when he found out nobody lived in any of the apartments. To make matters worse, the owner is reluctant to let him rent one. Eventually he negotiates an apartment in the historic old house, but soon finds out that he's not quite as alone as he thought. What ghostly secret has the owner failed to share?

It's up to Bud to unravel the mysteries of the upstairs apartments, but is he really ready to find out the truth?

The Bitter Harvest

The year is 1825, and a small Native American village has lost many of its people and bravest warriors to a pack of Lofa; huge beasts humanoid in shape but covered with coarse hair. The creatures are taller than any normal man, and fiercer than even the wildest animal.

Rather than leave the land of their ancestors, the tribe chooses to stay and fight the beasts. But they're losing the war, and perhaps more critically, they're almost without hope.

The small community grasps for anything to help them survive. There is a warrior on the frontier known as Orenda. He's already legendary across the west for his bravery and honor.

Onsi, a young villager, sets out on a journey to find the warrior.

Orenda will be forced to choose between almost certain death, not just for himself, but also his warrior wife Nazshoni and her brother Kanuna, or a dishonorable refusal that would mean annihilation for the entire village.

The crucial decision is only the beginning, and Orenda will soon face the greatest test of his life; the challenge that could turn out to be too much even for a warrior of legend.